Small Town Roads

By L. B. Johnson
Edited by Stephanie Martin

For Mary Hardig—for your strength and your future.

Contents

Prologue

Isaiah 22:23: *I will drive him like a peg into a firm place; he will become a seat of honor for the house of his father.*

Summer is in full bloom as a silver-haired woman stands upon her porch in this small town and thinks upon a verse from the book of Isaiah. The driveway is glistening from a recent rain shower, as brief as it was warm, the cement assuming a patina that is mirrored by the hand-plastered walls of her home. Sunlight strikes the trellis in a dazzling splash and then darts over the colorful flowers that stand at quick attention waiting for the sun's acknowledgment. On the porch, a white muzzled retriever sleeps beside her, lulled by a gentle breeze as a solitary car drives by, almost in silence, as if respecting this peaceful time. The silver-haired woman has no desire right now to disturb her faithful companion, her joints tired and aching with arthritis, even as she admires the muscular definition of her arms, still strong from working in the earth.

She's lived here for what seems a lifetime, staying after her husband passed too early at age sixty-one, a lifetime of smoking taking him too soon. She has no desire to move closer to the big city, no interest in downsizing. Her niece and her nephews will take care of the house when she is gone, she and her husband not having been blessed with children of their own. All she has asked of them is that they leave the flowerbeds as they are, so the cycle of flowers continues long after she is part of the earth.

Each year the flowers return, whether the winter embraces them or neglects them, making a statement of endurance too abundant for the limits of human speech. Then, on one of these lazy weekends, she takes to the planting beds, removing weeds. By the evening the lawn is gaudy with the dead and the dying detritus of a past year. Along with the expired shoots of the previous year would be the errant plastic-wrapped flyer or empty soda can, tossed with a careless hand only to reappear with that first shout of warmth, released from the cold and the dark only to be resigned to it again, there in the recycling bin.

It's a tradition and a cycle, these little rituals of tending to her home, there in those days where doors still stand closed in the morning chill, the flash of a fire's hearth only a forgotten gleam on the window. As the flowers come out and grass is cut for the first time, other things emerge from the neighborhood. Small toys and bikes show up in yards as if left there in the night by some spaceship from another planet. Flags are carefully hung; down the street, a clothesline goes up.

The neighbors' yards here in this small town are much the same, even the overgrown house at the end of the street. The homeowner and the town council are in a permanent state of impasse as to who really has to mow the corner, dotted with colorful wildflowers splashed on the ground as if flung up by the spray of water a passing car would create. There's an old mailbox in the shape of an old car and several statues of Mary, mother of Jesus, looking at the grass with eyes that are either laying a blessing upon the land or providing a gentle rebuke to a yard gnome that looks on from another flowerbed.

She goes outside and grabs the mail, noting the envelopes that say "valued resident" and not Evelyn Ahlgren, tossing them in the trash.

She watches the new owner of the home across the street arrive, a young woman with strawberry-blond hair. She remembers her as the niece of Ruby, the lovely lady who lived there and who passed away a short while ago, and hoped she would stay rather than sell it or rent it. They met briefly when the young lady lived with Ruby the summer after her parents both passed before she left for college up in Chicago. Living in a town of a couple of thousand people couldn't be too exciting for a young person after the bustling adventure of school and the sights found in the city. The young woman seems intent on just getting her truck through the very narrow street and does not notice her. Evelyn lifts a weathered hand and gives the young woman a friendly wave, one that startles a bird perched on a shrub as its sharp, tiny cries fall away like flung confetti.

As she turns back toward the house to brew tea, she realizes she has watched these flowers come up for over forty years. She planted some of them as a young bride with others added by her friend Ruby. They still maintain that innocent picture of color and brightness that she has looked at through years of weariness and years of joy, a picture that on the threshold of her final years she sees no means to alter. God willing, she will be here after that ancient trellis has fallen to ashes; she has no desire to spend her end days in assisted living with a tiny cement patio and a garden beyond that is so ordered and sterile that there is no room in it for human curiosity.

She hopes that she will enjoy these blooms until they fade one last time—her bedroom window open to the garden, taking in her final breaths as the infinite air calls in the calming scent of blossoms.

As the sound of her new neighbor's vehicle fades into the distance, she is simply going to sit and enjoy some tea on the porch, looking at her bounty of blooms on this first Friday of the month. She hopes that she is here at this time next year and the year after, living fixed in the monotonous repetition of the flowers, the garden's living symbol of hope.

Evelyn watches her new neighbor as a U-Haul truck and another vehicle full of young people pull up to her long-time neighbor's house. "Good," she says out loud. "She's going to live in Ruby's house." She notices such things, especially as they involve old vacant houses, bearing the form of the formerly beautiful. She notices such places in the country: old empty barns, the houses of which watched over them, also long abandoned. The barns always caught her eye, some mystery there in their silent lofts, where among the beams and rough-hewn boards, life from venerable times was lived according to venerable ways, never to be seen again.

There are many reasons such places are abandoned—foreclosure and death the main ones—yet they remain vacant and fallow, someone's dreams perhaps tied up in probate or simply discarded, no one wishing to assume the burden of that which will take some care to make whole. She only stops to look at such places. Then, she drives down the road to her home, an older place kept in meticulous repair. The house is warm, the walls adorned with only a few photos of the past.

This morning, as she went out to water her flowers, outside the small rental home two doors down, which had been vacated last week, there were a couple of neat bags of trash. Lying next to them were two large pieces of cast-iron cookware. She takes a closer look; both were high-end brands, neither purchased cheaply. Both looked unused but had thick rust covering them. She picks them up and takes them home to examine and clean since they have obviously been left and the owners would not be returning for them. Once the rust is removed, the pans oiled and properly seasoned, they will look as if new and will last a lifetime. Someone simply did not know how to care for what they had and had casually discarded them. She shakes her head at how little this new generation seems to know and hopes her old friend's niece is more level-headed.

As she watches the young people carrying the boxes into Ruby's old home, she thinks back to her life in this small town and recalls all of the things that happen here that go unseen or, at the very least, unspoken.

Out at the rural airfield, a man who still wears his youth in his eyes arrives for a local flight. He notices, off in the distance, tires flat, grass growing up into the wheel pants, an old tailwheel airplane sitting desolate. The paint hasn't seen a wash or polish in years; the once-bright hues that flaunted their color against the sky like a cry of a challenge now lying mute upon the grass. The engine that once fired up with life, growing louder and louder as the entire aircraft trembled like a racehorse waiting to run, lay quiet but for the rustle of birds who have built a nest in the intake. He wonders what it would cost to buy it, to get it flying again.

So many things go unnoticed until they are gone. Some lie barren, covered in days until they no longer shine, forgotten. Other things capture the eye of someone, be it a house, a piece of machinery, or an entire manner of living, which for that person possesses a life all of its own as it lives once more in their care. It is that missing piece of history, that forbidden apple whose taste could open up the pathway to heaven or cast one from all that is paradise. Yet they could not resist taking the challenge, like partaking of the fruit of the tree in the Garden of Eden, such things being fraught with the possibility of the undiscovered.

An elderly man sits alone in a house that still shows the remains of the recent past among the modern updates, the 70s retro hunters' blaze of orange touching some things like a flame, shag carpeting stamped flat by the trails of children past. It is quiet now, his wife and his only son preceding him in death. The TV is off, the windows open, the curtains breathing in and out with the soft exhalation of the evening. It is a night for memories or passages, those moments within us that by our history and remembrances release us from the shadows, our soul freed there in that one moment that makes certain silences clearer than any words that could be uttered.

In another home, one that's seen several generations come and go, a young man in a blue button-down shirt sits in a chair, surrounded by books and antiques. Each piece was carefully picked from the flotsam and jetsam of estate sales, carefully cleaned and placed in the room using only muscle and sweat. The safe, hidden in another room, holds a small collection of rare and unique firearms, some dating back to the Civil War.

Some people are born out of their due place, fate casting them too soon or too late, but they only look ahead, even as they bear a yearning for a place they knew not. On the shelf is a picture of an older woman with young eyes that look just like his. He looks at the photo, tracing the leather of the spine of a book, with hands that remember.

Across from Evelyn's house, a strawberry-blond-haired woman works in her basement, putting boxes away from the moisture, water having crept in during recent storms. In watching her work, you would think her to be a young girl. Only in the harsh light from the window do you know she is a young woman. She looks down at her hands and her forearms, the scar on her palm where she took a fall out of a tree, and the rough-edged dimple on her arm, where bone forced its way through when her first childhood experiment with gravity went awry.

There are other scars you could not see; the loss of her parents and a brother, but she foraged on, hoping to find something in this small home she inherited from her aunt, a place that holds memories visible only to her. She will not cry, even though she doesn't know a single person here. No, she's descended from immigrants and warriors; for her, life is simply a battle fought, the scars simply marking the skirmishes won.

She is moving some boxes and hanging bags, military uniforms, and gear, worn by grandfathers and beyond, men who are now only dust and remembered for their courage. There is a new box to add to these, for which she must make room. She opens the box, carefully packed up just a week ago to be moved; the uniform items carefully shrouded and laid to rest within. She touches them gently, and even in their stillness comes a moment of real and profound intimacy with the one who once wore them, unexpected and lasting, as is often our glimpse of truth. They will be carefully packed again to protect them and stored with those uniforms of generations past.

At the bottom of one box, carefully enclosed in bubble wrap, is a single toy soldier that had been unearthed in the garden one spring, years after the battle for world dominion with two children and their troops had ceased. The touch of its small battered form brought back the scent of the earth in their back yard, the shade of the apple tree that sheltered them, the warmth of the sun, times when she could ask Mom and Dad almost anything, and they'd tell her the truth.

Was this little figurine simply a forgotten toy or was he buried in some forgotten childhood military honor? She could not remember, but like anything long lost, he spoke to her of the reasons why we remember things and why they are important.

With the lessons of the past, we could live safer and smarter. We could make decisions based on what we learned the hard way, about the truth, about individuals, about intentions, those deceits, and traps that lay like spider webs for the naive or the unwary.

So she continues to look, sometimes seeing the past in front of her, in pieces found years after they were laid there, the answers beneath her hands under a mantle of dirt and time. She sees them sometimes late at night, out of the corner of her eye. Perhaps it's just fatigue, perhaps an awareness of more than these moments here and now but there, at the edge of her vision, she senses those moving moments of lives that went before. People who valued freedom over power, truth over political correctness, people unafraid to ask "why" or "how." People just like her, full of fear and pride and arrogance, courage and love, the knowledge of suffering, and foreshadowing of their death. They had been saying no to death for generation after generation, knowing that they could not stop it but damned if they won't go out fighting.

She sometimes looks into unseeing eyes, wondering if at that moment of their passing, the questions were answered, or if perhaps more compassionately, they had forgotten the asking of them. All that remains are scent and whispers there in that cold landscape, speaking and murmuring across time the questions they could no longer seek that she could give voice to with a simple but solemn signature at the bottom of an evidence document.

The items put away; she returns to a table covered with her dad's old tools, a place to work and repair, to form and craft. For, like her father, she finds something soothing in fixing and finding answers in that which was broken, even as she restores its use. Perhaps that's why after majoring in criminal justice she took a position as a police officer in this small town in which her aunt had left her a home, rather than seeking a forensic position in some big-city laboratory somewhere. Officer Rachel Raines. It had a nice ring to it.

Down the road, a young man in a button-down shirt picks up an old violin worth more than all of his other possessions combined, even though its appearance might label it in unknowing eyes as yard sale material. The notes reach out to the depths of the dwelling, penetrating the darkness, laden with the awe and enigma that could be borne on the strings of remembering men. From the shadows inside her basement, she hears the plaintive sound and smiles.

These people may all be strangers, or they may be bound by blood, bond, or friendship. They do share one thing: an understanding that life bears with it the remnants of the past. They could call it baggage or call it wisdom. They could cover it, shed it, walk away from it, forget it ever happened, and forget its lessons, but as they destroy that history, they destroy themselves.

Better they should preserve it for what it was—those moments, those things that made them what they are. They could treat it all as something shameful, or they could speak or write of it in a tone that would be a shout of triumph were the words on a keyboard capable of speech. They could live their lives, old before their time, for the burden of the past, or they could live sufficient and complete, desiring as the young do not to be bound but only to love, query, and scrutinize uncontested, left alone with their freedoms.

It is the future. It is the past. It is life in a small town.

As the vehicles across the street leave and lights come on upstairs in the long dark house, Evelyn sits in a chair, surrounded by books and antiques. The room has not changed since her husband died. On the shelf is a picture of a flame-haired woman and a handsome man. She slowly rises and walks toward it, joints stiff with pain, her form cleaving the space he once passed through. She passes a shelf, a book bound in leather, an old revolver, and a small vase, her glance touching what his eyes had lost. She picks up the photo and realizes that some things, even if not present, are never truly gone, fixed and held in the annealing ash that is our history.

As the night descends upon her unchecked, she stands and looks hard at everything.

Evelyn was up earlier than most people even though she'd been retired from her teaching position for three years. As the coffee pot came to life, she looks out on the faint bloom of trees outside the antique lace curtains, the tall branches of the oldest trees standing guard over tender young blooms, watching like sentient parents.

She sits behind an antique teacher's desk, in a heavy swivel roller chair that's easier on her old back than the kind she used when she was a teacher. On the desk are pencils and a brand-new laptop she is learning to use. Also on the desk are a coffee cup and some slightly crinkled papers that represented need and passion and the losses that sometimes had to be printed and held in hand to be fully understood, at least to her insurance company. In those papers somewhere was the truth, surrounded by verbiage, encompassed and encased by it. If she just stopped and let the words break free as the planet made just one more rotation, the truth would tumble from within like a shiny gem.

Then there is the house down the street that still sat dark.

The *For Sale* sign is still up, the yard tidy, the windows reflecting only that which is outside, nothing internal or intimate.

She just found that rather sad. The neighborhood was a stable one, the houses built many generations ago. In the last ten years, she had only seen one family move in on her block, outside of one rental home. That was due to a young couple taking advantage of a better job closer to parents in the state they were originally from and putting their home up for sale.

On the shelf next to her Bible is a rather old-fashioned but sturdy vase that had been her neighbor Ruby's. She'd bought it at a garage sale before Ruby died, as it matched the color of her wallpaper perfectly. She wondered if Ruby's house still had much in the way of furnishings in it. It didn't look like the young lady moving in had much furniture at all, and some of the original furnishings were sold when Ruby fell and then went into nursing care.

Outside of those two events, there's little change in the neighborhood. There are yellow ribbons tied to all of the trees at one home by the church where no movement is detected. The yard is occasionally mowed as the ribbons fade more and more each year, to where they look like tattered flags. There's a story there, one that would likely cut the heart like a knife. So many untold tales in these old homes of times and events that people met with either fear or courage; those times that try like stiffness and soreness of muscle or bone that some get so used to that they no longer notice the pain.

Such is life in a small neighborhood. The houses endure, as they have for multiple generations and will for generations more. People have losses and new lives, but there remains under these ancient trees a sense of continuity Evelyn would never get in the more modern subdivisions. With her husband's pension and insurance she could have sold this place and gotten a newer condo in a big city, but she chose not to. She prefers the stillness and the quiet of history while off in the distance cars rush on in a hurry. She read somewhere that all we have is time. It is true; this is the time between now and the death that we fear. People rush toward it, inventing new ways to do everything faster and easier, so that what time we have goes by in even more of a hurry until the clock suddenly chimes out our name.

A car pulls up, and the realtor meets a young man looking at the house for sale. She hopes it sells soon; seeing two dark houses on the street recently has been depressing.

Over at Ruby's, the downstairs of the house lies in darkness as upstairs the bright light from two small windows suddenly shines with the resilient hope of a lighthouse in a storm. She bets Ruby's niece makes that her office, as Ruby did, to better see all the flowers and trees from up there. Tomorrow she's going to fill that antique vase up with flowers and take it over to the young lady — Rachel, she thinks her name is — as she welcomes her to the community.

Chapter 1

————— ✳ —————

Dear Diary:

Is that how online journals are supposed to begin?
Where do I begin? I'm not even sure why I'm doing this as I have no family and no one is going to read this. However, I need something to do as I'm living in a new town (is this place even big enough to be called that?), my boyfriend just dumped me, and I'm starting a new job that I have no idea I'm even going to be good at.

When I sat down at this upstairs desk, I looked outside, and there were so many pretty flowers, especially at the house across from me where I think an older woman lived. I didn't know if she was married or widowed. In the city, while I was going to college, you didn't make eye contact with the neighbors, let alone get to know them. With all the crime, you never trusted strangers.

I intended on staying in the city, as dangerous as it could sometimes be there, because there was so much to do. There were parties, museums, stores, and big libraries; I was never at a loss for something to do. They were things that would keep me from thinking about things I didn't want to, like how I ended up orphaned so young, why my brother had to go and die from cancer when he was supposed to help me deal with Mom's early-onset Alzheimer's, and Dad's passing. Not to mention that my boyfriend suddenly decided he didn't want a life with someone who wanted to work in law enforcement. I think it was because I was four years older than he was, and I was growing up, and with growth comes change and a bigger awareness of the world. He just wanted to party and have fun just as I realized I needed to put that behind me.

That changed when my Aunt Ruby died.

Her small house stood on an even smaller lot, among a cluster of homes that went up when World War I ended and so many young men came home to settle down. There were dozens just like it, neat and ordered, awaiting those who survived to light their rooms with freedom. The house stood there, a hundred years later as around it, other homes popped up in open fields after the next Great War. It is surrounded by a variety of older homes; some farmhouse style and some bungalows, painted a variety of colors—a stark difference from the bland homeowner-association-approved blues and grays that loomed like Easter Island statues in the modern subdivision where I grew up.

It was my aunt's (my dad's older sister) house where I had spent many wonderful days as a child with my older brother during summer vacation exploring the tiny yard and garden while the adults sat in the tiny living room, sipping cold tea and listening to music from another era. I lived in this house as well that summer after Dad passed, nowhere else to really go in those brief months before I started college.

Friends had urged Aunt Ruby to sell her house when my uncle passed away years ago. Because of its location, in a small rural farm town, the tiny spot of land wasn't worth much money, and she didn't want to leave it anyway.

Change your life, they say. Get out from under your house and get a condo; forget your garden and your flowers and you'll have more freedom and money. The change would be good.

My aunt would have no part of it, and for that I was grateful. She continued living in that house with the same furniture she'd had as a young bride. In the house were also photos and books from their trips around the country, small excursions that only slightly dulled the pain of not being able to have children of their own. When I was a child, the furniture looked old and shabby, but as an adult, I noticed what she had. What she had was finely-made pieces of wood, made with real craftsmanship, rugs intricately woven and meticulously clean. She also had a collection of glass pieces as clear and flawless in vision as I've seen in my generation. They were things of quality; things worth saving.

Some of the furniture was sold when she broke her hip and had to go into a nursing home twenty-five miles away, but her big antique bed, her upstairs office desk, and the beautiful dining room set and buffet were still in the house as well as most of her kitchenware.

I never thought I would be living here; I never imagined she would leave the house to me though she left her meager savings to the church, knowing my parents had left me enough to finish school if I got a job during summer breaks. I wasn't a teen; I was well into my twenties since I put college off for a few years to take care of Mom and then Dad. I was anxious to get started with a life other than school.

I like being upstairs, being able to see out the window as I type these words.

Outside, in the late summer air, fog is starting to gather. A neighbor's car just pulled out, and it is moving into the bank of fog, disappearing as if it had never been. I wonder if that was the silver-haired lady that was good friends with my aunt; I think her name is Evelyn. That summer I was here after Dad died, I hadn't paid too much attention to others.

Where did that car go? To keep it in my mind's eye I had to draw upon memory and the echo of its passing. That's when I realized that all we have left of anything was the knowledge of what remained, even if you couldn't see or touch it; those traces that had value. You could lose everything—a house, family, or a loved one—and it's still there with you, reflecting your future, shaping your decisions, defining fury and grace, as you held on to that which made you strong.

My aunt knew that; not living in the past because she wasn't strong enough to move on and change her life, but taking from the past that which had value and using those things to validate the code by which she lived her life. Well-traveled, well-read, and having lived over eighty years, she understood that which went before us; events and words, action and men.

Whether we are rich or have a single possession to our name, we still have those best parts of our past. It's a voice on the phone, stories muttered by brave women and men, words on pages, and ideals passed on from one generation to the next. I had the stories of my grandfather and my uncle from World War II and Korea told to me generations after those battles ended. I had my uncle's wings from the Air Force. I had a small, crude cross my grandfather pounded out from a nickel on a long march during the war that broke most men. I have the history, the words of my nation, and those souls that founded and defended it.

Maybe that's why I never fit in with the University party crowd. I tried to fit in, doing all the dumb things like skipping homework, drinking alcohol, and using words you expect on HBO. Then one day I woke up with my late mom's words in my ear, *live your life to honor God, not yourself,* and I felt a bit ashamed as far as how I was acting. My parents had not raised me to be like this. I grew up with the notion that what was important was not your self-esteem or your popularity. What was important was self-respect, and that was something to be earned. My peers seemed mostly interested in themselves, even my boyfriend not understanding why I had decided I wanted to do something to help others rather than just get a job that would buy me lots of stuff. I had a couple of friends that understood how I felt and were raised as I was, to work hard and give something back. I hoped we would remain friends after graduation.

My aunt told me here in the summer after Dad died that her generation didn't have all of the things my generation does as far as educational assistance and social services, but what they had was the freedom to live; to make mistakes and grow. She told me I would learn that freedom was a lot more important than someone there to pick me up every time I faltered. I hope she was right, as now I wish there was someone here to give me a kind word since it's just me now in this house, all alone.

Oh wait; there's sweet tea in the fridge. And there's stuff to make nachos. OK, I'm not totally alone.

Well, dear diary, that's it for the night. I might continue our little talks in the future, but for now, I need to get to sleep as tomorrow's my first day on the job as a rookie police officer.

Chapter 2

————————✳————————

*T*he first day on the job went better than expected. I was happy to find out I didn't have to purchase my uniform as some small town police officers do. Unlike a bigger city's police department, once I have more training and experience I will likely patrol mostly alone. Living in a town where you pretty much know everyone allows me to feel not too worried. I learned that we spent a fair bit of time on public complaints, barking dogs, and fireworks, that sort of thing, and at least once a year there would be an incident at the pub involving a high blood-alcohol-content and tater tots that ended up with an arrest. Overall, violent crime was rare, but you still had to be on your guard.

Just because it's a small town doesn't mean it's completely safe. Having lived in the heart of the city the last four years, especially as a woman, I learned to be aware of what was going on around me. I listened to anything unusual, my eyes looking for anything out of order, a habit that was not out of fear but out of caution. I locked the door behind me, smiling in my freedom to live on my own, prepared and aware. I was always alert, even when the big city streets were quiet with snow blanketing the ground with the perception of purity. This was nature's design that hides the evidence of how the processes of life and death and predator and prey play out in both animal and human kind. I learned enough from my criminal justice major to know that predators would travel the roads and quiet fields of our life as long as there was darkness, the derisive echoes of their need carried out on the harsh wind. Even in this tiny town, out of habit, I looked around to make sure I was alone before heading from my truck to the house. As I moved toward the door, the air cooled my blood. The fields behind the town were empty and quiet, except for the steady sound of a small wounded animal somewhere in the distance, a constant cry into the wind.

In time I am sure I will relax more. This town wasn't Chicago, but it didn't mean there weren't people here that could wish to harm me, and I know that methamphetamine, otherwise known as meth, was a problem in any rural area in the country. That's not paranoid, that's just sensible, something even my aunt who loved everyone would tell me was smart.

Tonight when I got home I had two surprises. The first was that there were several cars in front of the empty house a couple of doors down that's for sale: an older but well-maintained van followed by a late-model SUV, driven by what appeared to be the parents of the young man looking at the house. The older woman went into the home with the realtor, while the men looked at the structural aspects of the house. I waved hello as I got out of my truck and went inside with my groceries for my first week here, glad to see someone interested in the place.

Then my neighbor from across the street came over with an old and clunky-looking green ceramic vase. It may have been ugly, but it was full of beautiful flowers. Evelyn also brought some homemade banana bread. I remembered her clearly now as a good friend of Aunt Ruby. She was widowed, although she didn't mention children, and had lived here since she was a young bride. She's old enough to be my mom, but somehow, I feel like she could be a good friend here, since many young people my age seem to have fled the area for the city. She said the vase was originally my aunt's, and I smiled, remembering it sitting on the buffet. It's rather ugly, but I bet that once it was considered beautiful. The gesture meant a lot, so I will make sure it goes up so she knows I appreciated it, as I don't want to hurt her feelings after she was so thoughtful.

The sunlight now is almost gone; there is nothing left but a bluish shadow that flows across the yards like moving water. As I type, I hear the cars down the street start up, headlights illuminating the deepening blue like a ship's lights. As they move away, a flock of birds takes flight with the movement up into the deepening azure; a thick swirl of shadows that wing off to places unknown.

I sit in what I've claimed as my office. Words spray out across the ether, my desk, and all its untidy clutter, fading into that anonymity of darkness as the day ends, and the only sounds are the tick of the keyboard and the soft, aimless tick of a clock.

Down the street sits that old, dark, and vacant house. Made of brick and wood, it held in suspension within its walls all of the fears, joys, and grievances that hearts broke for, many long since forgotten to dust. I don't know if the man that looked at it would buy it, but I pray that it will soon hold light, joy, and laughter again.

28

Chapter 3

———————✳︎———————

*D*ear Journal: I know we haven't talked in a while, but there was a good reason for that, which I will get to shortly. First, I have a question for you (as if you could answer):

Why didn't someone tell me that living in a rural area meant spiders the size of a Chevy Suburban?

When I got home, I picked up what looked to be a flier but apparently was the local newspaper. I thought I'd have a quiet evening. As I opened the door, a grasshopper rushed in. Huh? He was being chased by a very large spider. I got the door closed before I had a spider security breach, and then I captured the grasshopper in a jar and took him out to the safety of the back yard. After that I went and opened the front door again, since I forgot my suitcase in my truck. The spider was waiting, rushing at the door as if to say, *I Am SPARTA!*

Slam. OK, in the morning I'm leaving by way of the back door.

Hopefully, a family of giant spiders didn't move in during the weeks I was away at the Police Academy. It was longer than I thought it would be but the State Law Enforcement Training and Standards Board had pretty extensive requirements. I'm glad I'm officially an officer, although I'm on probationary status for a full year.

There was more to it than I expected. After the initial application, I needed to pass a written exam and physical agility test, the interview, the background check, a polygraph test and drug screening, the medical and psychological exams, and finally the training. Now I'm just learning the ins and outs of everything, taught by my fellow police officers.

I had already been proficient with a firearm, for this was something my dad had taught me as a teen. We usually had a firearm of some sort in our house and he wanted me to be able to handle one safely and responsibly. When I first started shooting, I would only be able to protect myself if I was attacked by a humpback whale, but by the time we were done with training, I could hit tiny targets accurately. I pray I never have to use this particular skill, but it's part of the responsibility we bear.

My colleagues were welcoming, and I was happy I wasn't the first female to serve in this town. It's a small force, even including our dispatcher and the administrative assistant. I'm definitely the youngest, so there's some ribbing about that, but overall everyone had been really nice. I know having my four-year degree in criminal justice helped with being selected as well as my family's connection to the town.

I need to explore the town a little better and find a place to get my hair cut. The only salon I've seen was on Main Street. It had those old 50s-looking driers, and most of the clientele appear to be retired ladies getting perms. I'm used to having my hair cut at the spa down the street in the city and don't want to go in there only to come out looking like a less gray-haired version of my aunt.

I love the quietness here, but I miss all of the amenities and businesses that were there in the city for the taking. For now, I need to make a quick phone call to let Evelyn know I was back, and add an offer to take her out to lunch as thanks for keeping an eye on my place. My neighbors said they'd pick up any newspapers or advertising flyers that showed up so it would look like I was at home and someone had cut the grass.

There in the living room in the vase that was a gift to me, the fresh flowers were all withered. Why did I think that vase was so ugly? The color was intriguing and familiar. I realized that it was the color of my parent's living room. It's not the green of the apples in the tree in the backyard, which hung low over the limbs we'd hang from like monkeys. It wasn't the deep gray-green swirl of a gentle river Dad would fish in. It was more of the color of aromatic sage that speaks of something wonderful coming from the oven; invoking memories of the laughter of Mom and Grandma in the kitchen; their recipes born of white paper and cursive script. It was the memory of those sounds that made me want to weep for the lost colors of childhood that resided in that one homey vase.

One last question, and then I am done. Why, if I am finally home, do I feel so homesick?

Chapter 4

———————❋———————

*T*his morning began with a distant rumble of thunder. I had a day off and had just snuggled down under the covers while the town slowly woke up outside. As the sky darkened, I gathered myself up to take a look at it, sharing something with the nature of that rumbling, as I checked the radar to make sure that rumbling didn't have rotation potential. Tornadoes are not uncommon in Illinois, and although I have a small walkout basement where the washer, dryer, and work tables are, I don't want to test its fortitude.

Last night's storms also accompanied me on a call out with Sergeant Beazly, one of the senior officers. I know eventually I'll be patrolling alone, but this first year I'm still the rookie and will be learning for a while. I'm trying to be the best I can be and learn quickly since I know it was difficult for a short-staffed department to have me gone for training all of those weeks.

We were sent out due to a call about a power outage which turned out to be caused by a car hitting a light pole, that meeting of car and pole being fatal to the young driver. Given my major in school, I'd seen plenty of pictures of dead bodies, but this was the first time I was up close and personal with one. I didn't know whether to cry or vomit, but I held it together. As the county coroner was called and the driver's license extracted from the wreckage so we could see who this poor soul was, lightning lit up the sky, laying bare all risks and renunciations, while we worked in the echo of someone's last whisper.

The storm rolled through fairly quickly and with quite a bit of rain. This had been quite the year for rain. I remembered all of the flooding I saw as I drove down to my aunt's funeral; whole farm fields were submerged, and others were dotted with large patches of dead vegetation that succumbed to days and days of standing water. The flat land was ridged and rutted with the marks of the centuries; the land passed over with wagons and guns, tears and tribulations. All laid bare by the deluge from above.

This morning, after a very long and emotional night on duty, I rose with the day and the sound of the rain and stepped out onto the porch and looked at the sky. The sun had come up in the east already; the horizon gleamed as if lit by a candle within, my form only a solitary sentry who forever challenged it.

It was only a few years ago that we had a drought; I remember the corn dying across the landscape. There was no pattern to it, no predictability beyond a farmer's almanac and the scattering of bones across the ground. I remembered one day that summer when I was out for a drive, not speeding, just cruising, and a cat ran in front of my vehicle. I had no time to react, but I had too much time not to do the right thing. I got a box and a little towel from my truck. I then placed the poor creature's covered form in the box and went to the door of the little farm house next door.

The woman that answered the door knew why I was there, having heard or seen the accident even as she looked past me as if hoping I'd disappear. I know I'm supposed to say, "I'm so very, very sorry," but I could not. As I set the box down, I simply stood there crying like a small child as she grabbed onto me like a lifeline, breaking into tears. She couldn't have been much more than a hundred pounds and felt like a bundle of sticks against my muscled form as she cried; sticks that had weathered very much for many years, only to be tossed onto a fire. I could offer no healing rain.

Last night, one of the officers and the Chief had to make that notification, but it would be for a soul much larger than a pet cat, as he informed a family that their son would not be coming home. I'm glad they didn't send me on that; I just don't think I'm ready.

For some reason, I thought of that today, as the rain dropped down on roofs that have wept the tears from above for well over a century. The town itself is old. About half the homes and outlying farms are a hundred years old or more. As I walked outside, trees that had existed long before I did covered my shadow. It's a quiet place and a safe area to walk. It's something I find myself doing on my days off. As I started off down the block, a flock of Canadian geese flew overhead, causing me to look up to a gunmetal sky as I looked around the neighborhood.

The wooden steps of Aunt Ruby's house tilted ever so slightly, as if tired. This was a project to be handled after I've managed to save up a little of my paycheck. Branches of age-old trees moved in the wind, and a flutter of birds were released as they bowed down upon the altar of a neighbor's porch. The air within was still with the invisible memories of the several generations who had likely lived in that home.

I wonder, if I could instantly take myself to this spot fifty years in the future, would it be the same? Would it even be here? That's something I will likely never know, as the future, like beauty itself, floats and is fleeting, undefined, and half-hidden in the quiet, still air, to be recognized only when we are ready. I moved here because my aunt was the only tie I had to my family and childhood memories, and it was one place I felt like I belonged. I still missed the city and my friends. There's fast food and speed dating; everything happening here and now. In contrast, life here was like a long nap. There was a church within walking distance, but I haven't been to church since Mom got sick. Perhaps I should go, at least once, to introduce myself.

I've yet to make any friends my age; maybe I'll ask the nice lady across the street if she wants to come over for dinner tomorrow. After living on college food for years, I'm ready to make an old fashioned pot roast and mashed potatoes.

Chapter 5

---❉---

*D*inner last night with Evelyn was more fun than I expected. I'm glad she picked a day later in the week when I invited her, so I had time to put it together. I enjoyed her company. Like my mother, she had a keen sense of humor and loved my book collection, offering to bring me some old books of hers to read. She is also of Swedish heritage as Mom was.

I can't afford cable quite yet, so I'm limited to a few Chicago channels I get with the antenna, which seems to consist mostly of bankruptcy attorney commercials and reruns of crime shows. So far the only "crime" I've had to deal with in my new job was a GPS stolen out of an unlocked car at the local gas station while the driver was inside paying for his fuel. The thief likely wasn't a local. With a town that's only a few hundred acres, GPS was not exactly something everyone was longing for enough to be willing to commit a crime for.

I didn't burn the pot roast, and Evelyn brought over some homemade lemonade that we enjoyed with the meal. She also didn't tease me about getting packaged mashed potatoes. Instead, she excitedly said, "just like Mom used to buy!" I just didn't want to get the huge bag of potatoes which was all our local small grocers offered. No individual ones were in sight in any of the bins.

There was one awkward moment. I went to dive into the potatoes, and Evelyn looked at me very carefully and said,

"May I say grace?" I blushed for a moment and then nodded yes. Why was that hard? My parents bowed their heads and said grace before each and every meal, even in restaurants. How had these last few years taken me so far from that? It wasn't just the partying in school; it was stepping back from all that I grew up with. I was finding the memories to be so painful. I was surprised that when Evelyn held my hand as she prayed, I felt a familiar comfort. God hadn't been anywhere while I checked out; He'd been with me all along. I just needed to learn to talk to Him again.

Because it was dark, I walked her home, just to make sure she got inside safely. She teased me about fussing over her, but if she was my mom, that's what I would have wanted someone to do. She also said she'd introduce me to her niece, a nurse who was about my age and lived in Brownstown, the little city less than an hour south of here. Perhaps she and I could be friends and make some trips to Chicago together.

As I returned to the house, I took my boots off, gliding quietly over polished floors, throwing my denim jacket on the fragmentary curve of a chair. The house quiet now, I went down to the basement, ducking my head in courtesy to the low ceiling, where I would take up a tool and hammer my loneliness into a piece of wood. I think of the homes I had lived in. There were two during childhood, all now gone, now inhabited by strangers who probably painted over the sunny rainbows I always had on my walls.

I didn't know if I wanted to live in such a small town for more than a few years, but there were memories here. The china we ate off at Thanksgiving remained in the cupboards; my uncle's books still sat on their shelf. There, in the closet, were the carefully-tended uniforms of a Great War, the cloth itself assuming the shape and form of those who are our heroes. It loomed tremendously against that backdrop of books, tools, and a small folded flag whose presence filled a sleeping house.

I opened up the window, the air breathing in and out. Lightning again flashed, and with the weight of the dark my breath quickened; my blood was running warm and quiet. So many places are now gone or changed that what I remember of them was more like recalling a piece of music I've heard but never played.

I couldn't sleep last night. My eyelids twitched as I tried to sleep, the movement in response to my brain's thoughts or perhaps merely the cyclical movement of the earth and all of her angels above. In this place, there were memories made, and life was perhaps forever changed.

I wondered, if years from now I moved back to the city, would I drive by here, just to see if the memories were still here? For our homes are often the places of our happiest memories. They were scraps of time, like scraps of a note where your name once lay; it was a bit of stiff paper that meant little by itself yet was still kept. You would not burn it or throw it away because it meant something, something you could hold even if the marks upon it were faded to white, something that said what you were. Something that said what you felt, even as you still are in some way the same.

After hopefully many years of dreaming and growing, there will come another night with eyes that twitch with the mind's flooding, even if the body is failing. The eyes are full of everything, save consciousness, and others gather around, looking on with knowing and unbearable eyes. The places of your memory are likely long gone; all that you have here are the pictures of them in that brain that still sparks like a match, unspoken stories mirrored in the eyes of those around you in your last days.

Those places are never truly lost. They simply lie near a peaceful trail, beside a placid and assuring pond of spent years' remains, in the mirror of days in which the mind still contemplates older desires and everlasting hopes. They are there, always quiet, musing, and steadfast, the joy still triumphant even if the actual place is now cinder and dirt. In that brain was one final vision, a place perhaps, a person, someone for whom that spark still exists even if they were years gone. As the breath slows, the body remembers, and the eyes finally close as they embrace the all-seeing.

Since I couldn't sleep last night, I did something I never could do in the city after dark; I went for a walk, though I was armed just in case I came upon a rabid cow or something. As I walked past the old cemetery, I noticed a floral spray on one of the new graves. It was from the funeral of the young man who lost his life the other night in the car crash. Much of the town was there at the funeral as well as most of the officers, paying their respects to his grieving family. He's not the only young person that is buried there; automobiles and farm machinery have a way of being unforgiving. I note another marker for a young man buried before he was even eighteen years old. It was erected long before the soul's shroud that lies beneath would have believed, a life cut short without pattern or prediction. The stone had seen both sun and rain. It had witnessed the dry heave of grief coming deep from the chest and the splash of tears against stone. It will be here as the landscape grows, withers, dies, and grows again, generation after generation, even as those who visit fade from drought to dust. It will be here when the night calls our name and doesn't look back.

I arrived back home without making my journal entry, and, with my jacket put away, I fell asleep on the couch I'd picked up at a rummage sale, wearing my aunt's fluffy bathrobe that still smells faintly of Wind Song perfume. At first light, I awoke. From outside the window, the rain ceased as a flock of geese flew overhead. Their sounds rose toward an astonishing crescendo, beyond the compass of hearing, as they flew upwards into a bright blue sky.

Chapter 6

———————✳———————

$\mathcal{T}$he silver-haired lady across the street watches as a car pulls in and later, after supper, sees the upstairs light of her new neighbor turning on. *Rachel is home.* She wonders why her young neighbor gravitates to the upstairs office each night. She most likely has online friends, or perhaps she just likes to write down her thoughts.

She knows she is not elderly by any means, but she seems to have taken on the role of caretaker for many of her neighbors since her husband passed. She is a strong, proud woman, and though her husband was the spiritual leader in their home, her joy, and her example, he valued her opinion and made her a part of each household decision that affected both of them.

She worries about the young woman that's moved in across the way. She's obviously very bright; that was evident in their first meeting, but she wears a mantle of sorrow that is heavy upon her shoulders. She can't imagine what it would be like to lose one's whole family at that young age. It's made her wise beyond her years, but she still carries grief as a child does, fresh and raw.

She also recalls the look in Rachel's eyes the other night when she asked her to pray with her. It was as if it was foreign to her, yet when she began that old Lutheran prayer for dining, "Come Lord Jesus be our guest; and let these gifts to us be blest," Rachel immediately, but softly, said the words along with her.

She would not pry, but she hoped Rachel would open up to her as to why she had closed off her heart to the Lord.

She can't help but think of Rachel not as a grown woman but as that little strawberry-blond child that visited that home in the years before she came to live with Ruby, after her parents passed. Rachel's companions during that stay were the books she coveted. They were things that she did not so much simply love but craved like an addict, such as the fire that flowed from the writer's mind through fingertips to be burnt upon the page, then doused with the water of laughter or tears and wrung out again. Ruby always said there was no interrupting her when she was like that. The house could burn down around her as she embraced the words even among the flames. She remembers Ruby saying, "She'll love everything that hard. That will be both her blessing and her curse." She wonders why she remembers it so strongly.

For now, she had others to concern herself with.

Next door to her, an elderly man sits in front of a cold television set; the house is warm but silent this day. There are plenty of homemade meals, frozen and carefully put away and labeled, made both by his neighbors and by a young lady that works as a part-time nurse's aide for him. Tonight, he could probably use some company along with some home-made chicken soup, something familiar and warm for his soul on this fall day.

Outside, the wind blows, the remaining leaves clinging to mostly bare branches as fiercely as flags. Evelyn picks up the phone to call him. She's seen lights go on and off, yet she had not seen him go outside for a walk, something he enjoyed even in the cold, and she was a little worried.

He was glad she noticed.

His son used to live there with him while the son battled cancer, and she remembers those last days. His son was sleeping even early in the day and taking in little nourishment, besides that which is needed for breath. The two of them had some adventures there in those days after the chemo was done. It was a brief period of endless times tearing up the streets, if only in the form of a road trip or two, a huge bottle of pickled herring, a six pack, and a trip to the ER in the little city that's twenty-five miles away because someone got bad acid reflux. Evelyn remembers visiting him at the hospital and chiding him on his behavior even if both of them laughed about it. Good times; times winding down, they both thought, while they watched his son sleep most of the day as if the heavens forgot to wind him up to continue living.

Tonight, his son is gone, and his wheels are silent. She's going to go on over with some supper and let him talk out his memories. He, in turn, is glad he has neighbors that check on him and the nurse's aide with him in the morning and at bedtime. He is a man that's already outlived his wife and his son, been part of a Great War, and watched his friends die, limping back from battle in an aircraft punctuated with German greetings. He's as tough as some winter hardy plant that can bloom under the heel of snow, unaware of the heart's unceasing combat with its thinning blood

Evelyn knows her neighbor would not have given up the experience of adopting and raising his son, for any happier ending. As she made her plans to spend some time with him, that's what she will remember.

Before she leaves, she goes back inside her little office and pulls out a photo that's not on display. It is a picture of someone in a nurse's uniform, not here, but always present. It is her niece whom she loves like a daughter. She feels a certain comfort in knowing that for now, at this moment, their world is quiet. There's a certain warmth in knowing that someone you love is safe. They do not need to be present for that feeling to exist. The feeling is like a wet finger on a burning wick, hot, but not scorching, possessing a slow, deep solidity of heat that only the tragedy of time's cessation would truly extinguish.

Soon she is knocking on her neighbor Harry's door, with food, with care, with prayer, making sure he's not alone tonight. He looks through the peephole, unlocks the door, and opens his home and his heart; it is all that is left to him. In his closet is a military uniform, on his porch an American flag, and within his reach, until he is too frail to handle it, a shotgun that had fed and protected him for over seventy-five years. On the table is a photo of a tiny spitfire of a woman, years before her bones shrank inwardly, her mind and her flesh growing sparse in those last days—a woman whose side he never, ever left.

We love with great depth, we defend with great pride, we protect with a generation's honor, while we always keep our guard up, our eyes open equally to worry and wonder.

Chapter 7

———— ❋ ————

*D*ear Journal: I am getting my bookshelves filled up. I probably should have kept some of my college textbooks, but I needed some cash while I went through the Police Academy, so I sold them. I only had a few paperbacks and no TV in the house when I first moved in (thanks, Aunt Ruby—that Victrola is going to be *so* entertaining when I finally make friends here), so I needed some more books. I have since found a small used television set, but I still prefer to read.

I love to read as much as I think I like this whole keeping-a-journal thing. It's different than in my mom's day when it was "dear diary" in a little book kept locked and hidden away from your siblings. Now I just turn on the computer and write about my day, and then I curl up with a can of soda or some tea and a book. I don't know what I'd do without my books. Remember the book *Fahrenheit 451* by Ray Bradbury? It was set in a dystopian future in which firefighters intentionally burn any house in which a book was located because it's illegal to possess them. In the end, a fireman who secretly grew to love books escapes the city of big screen, reality-based entertainment, to find a small group of book-loving refugees banded together. Each person was assigned the memorization of one complete book—including Plato, Dickens, James Joyce and more—so the books will survive until society is ready to posses them again. I loved that book when I was in high school. I did not read a lot of popular novels, though I had a rather large collection of classic literature while growing up. When my grade school classmates were reading and loving their mysteries or the *Captain Underpants* series, I was reading Jane Eyre and Henry David Thoreau, and a whole world beyond my quiet, hushed one at home opened up to me.

Maybe I should have majored in English, as words were so special for me. I also wanted to get a good job when I graduated, and with everyone and their brother writing books now, I knew I likely would never have a career as a writer. Let me just be the good guy, get the occasional cat out of the tree with the fire department, and ticket that obnoxious guy in the Buick that called me "sweets" when I gave him a ticket for speeding in the school zone while my training officer looked on.

Reading is, for me, not just intellectual but physical. I love the way the spine of a book feels in the crook of my fingers; the smooth, hard end boards snug on either side of the pages sewn together, their edges flush and perfect. I totally lose track of time when I read. I read somewhere that time, as most of us think of it, is an illusion; the past, the present, and the future are here, now, captured in a touch, the blink of an eye, or perhaps, simply between two pages of a novel. Today, between two pages of a favorite book, I found a photo of Mom in her garden. Outside the window here now, a plant waits for spring, when it can spill forth its seed onto the soil. I remember days of working in the flowerbeds that my mom so lovingly maintained.

After her death, I kept it going as long as I could for my dad until he too was called away. As I toiled in the garden, the sun kissed the top of my head, the touch a benediction, a blessing.

I missed having a big used bookstore a bicycle ride away, but there were often yard and garage sales here in town, and I could often find old books for just pocket change. The last time I was at a used bookstore, I found an old cookbook, two generations old, that I opened to browse and purchase. I could picture my aunt using a book like that, and I thought it would look nice on the shelves with the books that remained in the house. In it was a dried flower carefully pressed within the pages so many years ago.

I have many books like that old book, purchased from stores that contain more light than dust, containing within them things old and forgotten, things that in the wrong hands would only grow older. Finding the right one was like finding treasure. Fingers trace the spine, fingers that are gentle and forgiving, not wishing any further scarring upon that which binds. Such books find their way home, where they are pulled out to be read on late nights, the mind marveling that other minds marveled; the mysteries and the mistakes play out across the pages as if they were penned today. They tell their stories like some old and lonely shut-in would do to anyone who was willing to listen; lessons are given without rancor or heat. There are so many words that need to be said while they can still be heard. I always make sure I have a book with me when I travel.

The one time I took a really long trip in college with a school group overseas, I had to downsize a bag as the little turboprop airplane, being piloted by who I believe was The Incredible Hulk, was weight restricted, and my books were left behind for materials I had to have for the school trip. I almost would have rather given up my lunch, my poncho and my hiking boots instead of my little collection of paperbacks and a small leather-bound book of Shakespeare sonnets. Let the weather wreak havoc on my itinerary, let the grocers sell the last chocolate bar, but if I were to end up alone in the middle of nowhere after I bust a move down the Himalayas and break my leg, I wanted a book.

Curled up in strange places next to an artifact of the family that is toted around in my suitcase, I might be lonely, but I would be content. For I have a book. It's a big old, paper-made, dead tree book. I want to hold something in my hand that feels alive to me, even if a living thing died to create its pages. There are words that form pictures, laid out upon a living thing that never slept, never dreamed of the soft perch of birds or the sharp blade of the ax, and never mourned the tender leaves that it nourished and abandoned. It's a piece of wood that could be warmth, support, shelter, or the perfect, pristine bed of memory laid down bare.

I was alone, not having met any women my age yet, only sweet Evelyn across the street. She had been a high school English teacher so perhaps she'd like to read some books together. My house was empty, but I was not lonely tonight. In my head was history and the cries of warriors, rushing forth immortal beneath disported sabers and brandished flags, and there were men rushing forward into time, propelled by gunpowder and righteousness, underneath a sky of thunder. I have a book. I am caught up in battles and loves, both forbidden and forgotten, coursing like blood as long as the words will—that immortal, fresh, abiding blood which bears respect above regret and commitment above the ease of dishonor.

My housework is going to be put aside for at least an hour or two before bed, and I'll pick up that book. I'll let it transport me to somewhere far away until a chime will toll for warriors, for battles won and those so easily lost. As my hand turns the pages, I will move among people who lived and died, or perhaps never existed at all, their shadows not of flesh or blood but imagination, shadows as strong as finely-honed steel and shadows as quiet as murmuring breath, forgotten until they were put upon paper. Then, upon hearing the sharp, clear and quiet blade-like sound of that chime, perhaps a clock, perhaps something that just travels within me, I will fall off into sleep. The book lays prone on the nightstand next to me. The book and I are two forms, creating one shadow. The stories in both of us never cease, even at rest. Outside, the world continues in that illusion of change, the sky letting go of its tears, washing a parched landscape anew.

Chapter 8

———— ❈ ————

*Y*es, oh Journal, I know I've ignored you for the past few weeks, but life was getting busy again. Still, I committed to documenting my first year here, if only for myself to read someday to any future kids I may have.

Evelyn and I were still enjoying getting together to talk about books. Maybe someday I'll let her read one of my entries here. She was an English teacher, so she'll probably tell me, "don't quit your day job," but I really enjoyed having a creative outlet in a life that was seemingly so structured.

Well, not always structured. Yesterday, my day started at the police station with a very intoxicated woman calling from California to say that her ex-husband threatened to beat up her new boyfriend. I asked for her former husband's name. When she told me, I asked if she meant the son, as there was a Jr. by the same name. She responded, "no—HIM." The gentleman in question was in his 80s at least and uses a walker. We've never had any dealing with him other than seeing him at the diner, as he remained happily single after their divorce forty years ago according to the locals. Then both of them got on Facebook with the help of the grandkids. Apparently, out of curiosity, they checked out each other's pages and in a jealous fit, according to the complainant, he allegedly "threatened her ninety-year-old boyfriend." I looked at the "threat," and it consisted of, "He looks like a sissy boy, I could take him any day," which is really more an insult than a threat, so I told her to call back when she had more credible information or less alcohol in her system.

Then I did a routine traffic stop that didn't go as I planned.

You see, after being here a couple of months, not including the time at the academy, I finally got asked on a genuine date. It was the handsome fellow that manages the local hardware store. I was in the store, out of uniform buying some construction supplies and he asked if I'd like to have coffee at the diner after he got off work tomorrow. Then we could drive to a town that had a movie theater with his sister and her husband. He was a local who I did not recall seeing a mug shot for, so I figured it was safe to go out with him. Having spent months alone after Dan and I broke up, I was elated.

He was less than elated when I pulled over his car for speeding that evening, to the point that I couldn't let him off with a warning.

There was no date.

I called Evelyn and told her that she better live a long time because I'm going to become a crazy cat lady, living alone in that little house, which, being a dog person, was a real personal conflict for me.

She just laughed and said, "he'll come along when you least expect it."

I decided to go work off some of my frustration in the basement, as I was trying to build a small table from plans that seemed to have been translated from a foreign language the writer didn't speak. Either that or they were secretly planted by the particle board furniture store south of here to get us to drive to a bigger city to buy stuff rather than craft our own.

I enjoyed the work, the tools, and my hands speaking without sound, as animals do. It was a movement of efficiency and motion, a structured rhythm that brought order to an otherwise crazy day. We all have tools we use more than others. Some collections are extensive; some are just a couple of simple items.

My house was filled with old tools, since the garage and work bench were actually used for work. There's a bit more than just the hammer and screwdriver. There's a belt sander. When hand sanding is not enough, this handy little electric job could turn a minor touch up job into a complete home-finishing project as quick as you could say, a la George Jetson, "Jane—*stop* this crazy thing." There were several saws, including one that was the Congress of tools. It starts with a good idea and a straight course, and then it turns every which way due to lack of direction and a tendency to lean to the left, ending up with something that doesn't even begin to look like the original plan. Of course, there were lots of vice grips that make excellent branding tools when heated up during a welding project.

I remember Dad being out in his shop in the garage on the weekends, the sound of a saw, the beat of a hammer, as he was fixing up things to make our lives more secure. Dad could craft or fix anything that was made out of a tree, raising his hammer above something old and weathered like a new flag above a vanquished fortress.

My brother and I used to just sit and watch him, happy to be in his company while Mom was busy with ironing or working on her crafts. My own weekly chores done, I'd be quiet, looking at the light coming in from the single garage window, the glints and glares upon whirring metal, the sunlight like sparks upon my dad's hands as they worked.

One day Dad said, "Let me show you how to do something," and I knew better than to question him, so I simply watched and learned.

To Dad I was always going to be "his little girl," but he understood my inquisitive mind, even then. He was also mindfully aware of his mortality, having had an earlier, mild heart attack before the one that took him, determined that when he was no longer there to protect me, I would have the mindset to put up my tools and save myself.

I learned about safely handling tools and what was used for what purpose. We built our own little things: a flower box, a birdhouse, and some soap box derby cars with my brother. Once we took two very large sheets of plywood, sanding them and painting them green. Topping some saw horses, we now had a base for Dad's old Lionel trains that took over the garage on the weekends, working together out in the garage as if our forms were joined by some mechanical arm. We'd work until my arms ached, fading light drowsing on the floor like a drop cloth, slowed down by fatigue but still inevitably moving.

Not many people know how to build anything these days or take the time to craft. We go to a store and buy disposable things made of an often inferior material, to be cast aside before the next generation was even asking to borrow the car. Newness is often prized above quality, and pristine and perfect qualities are more valued than something you could stake your life and heart on, even if it had a few dings.

It's hard work, the tasks that we do to protect and provide for ourselves and our loved ones. There are fractured attempts and splinters, cuts and sharp edges, and sharp judgments, but it's rewarding work. For I enjoy such things, pulling cabinetry out of the wall, taking tools and making them do what I needed, the sweat on my forehead reaching my mouth, tasting of who I am: someone who's worked hard for everything she's got. Someone who raised some sweat to keep it; someone who could spill blood to protect it.

I learned that as I did necessary repairs on Aunt Ruby's home, where I worked late into the nights alone, putting whacked fingers to my lips, tasting air, life, and blood. I have used my brain, I have used old manuals of instructions, and I have used my dad's words. Yes, I was alone, using leverage to swing the tools, but at times it seemed like there were two of us: the tools and I, working side by side as if we were old friends who could guess each other's moves.

Outside, the first snowflake of the season drifted down. I put up my tools to make sure I had enough firewood handy in case the power went out, but first I had to make a quick stop in the bathroom to use the facilities.

As I entered the bathroom an enormous spider scurried across the floor toward me. Small spiders I'll carefully gather up and take outside, but this was one very large, very hairy spider, so I reacted on pure instinct, not wishing to be bitten in case he turned out to be a Brown Recluse. That meant throwing a hand towel on top of it as I performed my rendition of the *Grapes of Wrath* stomp.

Stomp Stomp Stomp.

Please be dead Mr. Spider.

There was no movement from under the towel. The spider didn't escape, as the floor around him was clean. I left him there, got my firewood, and went to bed after brushing my teeth in the other small half-bath upstairs.

This morning, I went to grab the towel and throw it in the wash when something caught my attention: the large dead spider was a few inches away with his legs curled up. He'd managed to crawl out and expire next to the tub, rolled up like a crescent roll. OK. At least he was dead. I went to get a paper towel to dispose of the remains.

This was where the fun started. When I got back, Mr. Spider was completely reanimated and angry, on *top* of the towel, ready to pounce on my foot like a Chihuahua dog on a pork chop. He had been dead; I'd been sure of it.

I had the only zombie spider in all of the Midwest. Fortunately, I'm a highly-trained law enforcement professional. I got a roll of paper towels and a can of Bug Stop.

Double Tap.

Chapter 9

Dear Journal: we are going to have the first big winter storm of the season.

It has been a busy couple of weeks. I've attended the church down the street, Lutheran, like the one I had been raised in. The people there were very welcoming, and it did not feel as odd as I expected after years of shrugging it off. They asked me to Bible study, but I politely declined, though I will think about it.

I was still lonely when I was home, even with the visits from Evelyn, so I went to the local dog pound and adopted a stray. He's a Labrador retriever mixed with a much smaller breed. He's stocky but had fairly short legs, with a perfect little Lab face. I named him Clyde. He just looked like a Clyde. Someone had found him wandering with no collar, and though he was in good health and had been neutered, he was hungry and scared. I got him up-to-date on his shots and was happy to find out he was house-trained. I wonder if he'd gotten away from someone that had been renting in the area as they were moving.

With Clyde safe and happily napping, it was time to get my latest journal entry done as our first major winter weather system was coming with a lofty and mighty sigh. Like death and taxes, you are not exempt. Depending on where you live, it may or may not include snow, but winter *will* arrive, not with a whimper, but a howl.

It's usually preceded by a trumpet of doom from the news channels which are often wrong. I had picked up a mostly-unused TV after I moved here, but I could look at the local radar on my computer to check the actual weather. At least that way I could see the severe weather coming while Accu-Hunch was predicting another six inches of sunshine, while on the days with great weather they're predicting doom and gloom. Sometimes the weather was boring and dressing it up with doom and gloom might have been good for the ratings. I don't think it does the unwary any good when an unreality was made a possibility, probability, and then a matter of fact, for no other reason than fear becoming words.

One does need to stay forewarned, though. On my lunch break yesterday, I took my truck and made a trip to the grocers for extra water and coffee and found the aisles clogged, not by the young, but by the middle-aged and seniors, buying extra bread, milk, water, and perhaps some firewood. I gave Evelyn a call to see what I could pick up for her. I wasn't surprised when she said she keeps lots of provisions, but she did say she wouldn't turn down some ice cream. It was cold enough it wasn't going to melt in the truck before I was off duty, so I snagged her some.

As I drove toward home yesterday, I could read all the markers in the sky, having grown up in the Midwest. It did not look comforting. Some storms you just stay away from. Others rose without forecast, especially coming down from the north. You might get a heads up in a monotone voice on the radio that warns of "rotational potential" in a tone that could just as easily be saying, "we're going to have to break that bone again." Other times it was simply "surprise!" as the sky became an angry mob of clouds.

In those moments, the sky could go from clear to a seemingly instant towering outburst of fury, as if all of the air had turned on you in confrontation, the tenuous earth only a memory beneath you. In what seemed like just minutes this morning, the wind suddenly picked up, and the patrol car—that seemed so sturdy when the drunk from the pub was beating on the hood late one night, thinking it was his car and that we were stealing it—now was tipping side to side as the wind tried to blow it over. I looked at people safely inside where it was warm and thought, *I could have been a CPA!*

So yesterday I looked at the sky with those knowing eyes, even if all I had to worry about was getting stuck waiting on a train between the station and home. As the signals come down, there was no worry, no schedule, only the wind that hit my vehicle broadside, rocking it ever so gently, as if it was a child's cradle. Now and then the sun peaked out, glinting beyond the clouds in swooping shafts that set fire to the tracks before they are doused in cold shadow again.

We had already received a pretty good surge of snow by the time I was off-duty. It was late when we had to deal with a man who had gotten his back wheels stuck and, in an attempt to get them unstuck, wore the tires down to the rims. That resulted in the arrest of said driver as he blew a 0.14 blood alcohol content. He was probably safer in jail last night during the cold than outside.

At home, the house was readied. There was de-icing salt by the back steps in a pet-safe bucket, and shovels for both the front and back porch. The flashlights were set out in easy reach, the beeswax candles available in each room, and an extra blanket was out for the bed, should the power go out. Then, lastly, the truck was moved to be just outside the back door. It will end up covered in snow, but the garage that I normally parked in front of was far behind the house, an ocean of cold darkness I didn't wish to tread in the dark, out of sight and sound of any neighbor, should I fall. It's just the dog and me, and we waited as the wind tapped at the door like an unwanted door-to-door salesman.

Night soon descended and the snow began to fall in heavy drifts. As it did, the sounds around me changed. I couldn't hear it within the house, but from the porch, as I let Clyde down the steps for his last pit stop, the town's main street a block away goes almost silent. What few cars are still out are enveloped by the snow, the screech of engine and tires muted to a few ponderous thumps as they drove over and past a little construction area.

The back landing, which I had shoveled, had a patina to it, like an old wall that had been plastered by hand. The trees were bare but for a brace of foliage that clung on with a death grip, screaming into the wind without words, plucked with a cold hand that tosses their cries to the ground like colorful scraps of paper.

I looked up before bringing Clyde back in. The sky was bright, as if illuminated from beyond. Another light is seen through this starry night, a night of wonders and far-away mysteries revealed for just a moment as the clouds break, a low crevice in the glittering ice cold that was space; a place where the earth was just one tiny fallen leaf whose cries only God could hear.

I couldn't help but think that I'm in some kind of cosmic snow globe, and as the porch shuddered slightly in the wind, I wonder if heaven had tilted the earth just a little to watch the flakes swirl around the lone form of one of its humble creations. I wonder if God could look down through that tiny fissure in heaven and see me down here, wearing my brother's old coat, pulling it around me for warmth that was beyond fabric or insulation.

I squeezed the salt out of my eyes as the light disappeared. For just a moment, there was no snow, no wind at all. A lull had come, the holding of a stormy breath, and I knew I had better get in the house now, the door now only a beggar's prayer against the incoming cold and wind.

57

Back inside, I shook the snow off my boots onto the entryway rug, the warmth wrapped around me even as the wind outside began to howl. I heard a voice outside the window as one of my neighbors, a retired Navy veteran, and his wife who moved here to be close to their son, a local farmer, let their dog out before the worst of the storm. I heard the bark of their dog as it was released, then the shouts as it's called back in from the yard, shreds and remnants of tattered shouting, snatched past the ear, followed by silence.

I gave Evelyn one last call to let her know I was OK and that I'd left her some ice cream in a bag on her porch. I knew my friend David from college would call. He and I were platonic friends from well before college. During my last two years of college, I had a boyfriend, and David was devoted to his studies, but we were often lab partners in chemistry, and we'd hang out at the library studying together. He was rather thin and shy with thick glasses that my boyfriend made fun of. David was involved with a Christian study group which I declined to join, but I enjoyed the friendship. We talked every few weeks, just sharing silly science jokes, and I knew if he saw the forecast he'd likely call me, as I kept my old cell phone number when I moved.

There were no further sounds from outside last night but the swooshing sound of a snowplow and the mournful cry of a police siren far away. I was really glad I wasn't on duty last night. From inside, there was only the tick of a clock. The silence was natural to me, in warmth and deep cold. It was a good night to sit with a mug of hot chocolate. The dog was curled up in his bed as I waited for the phone to ring. I missed my friend's voice, one that was not noise or a distraction; but rather the penetrating effect of quietness in the enormous din of noises, a small bit of peace beyond the dark ruins of the squall.

The first winter storm. By this morning, the temperatures were down in the single digits, and the back steps and landing were cleared again, subdued with salt. My breath caught in my throat as I took that first deep gulp before letting Clyde out in the back yard at first light. Like after a big rain, what I breathed in was fresh like that crisp metallic taste of the brittle air. The crust where the snow had frozen was whispering to me with the slow respiration of our movement, a faint crackle like something coming to life.

When I called for Clyde to come in from the fenced yard, my voice simply coiled out of the cold with sharp recoil that hung in the cold like an echo.

Sound was returning to the village. You could hear the hum of a snow blower, the scrape of a blade against a car's window, and the excited shouts of children a few doors down. The shadows on the snow appeared as if laid there by a stencil, the trees draping over them with their burden of white. From a distance, the bells call the faithful to worship, a long pull of sound dying away behind the trees as if it were echoing through another morning, another season, where part of you will always linger. Last night in emails I had the gentle comments from old classmates that started jobs down south, teasing me in regards to their warm temperatures and their lack of snow. As I was looking out at the Sunday morning landscape, washed clean in white while hearing the joyful shouts of the innocent in the air, I felt that I would not trade this for any spot of warm beach. Here in this thin, eager air, after the storm has passed, every breath is felt, every touch of warmth is savored. I understand, even in the cold, how lucky I am to be alive today, as I listen to the church bells, the sound of grace under a gentle shawl of snow.

Chapter 10

———————✳———————

*T*onight I first noticed the ambulance, coming up the street with lights flashing but no siren. Behind it was a police car, then another, also with no siren. It was the beginning of winter, and the windows fogged with the glow of the fire. The concentrated glare of those red and blue lights brought me to the window, my form as unnoticed as a mote of dust with all that was happening outside.

Such scenes are common in the big city, but not so much in this small and quiet neighborhood. There are injuries at home and an occasional heart attack. There's a rare break-in through a basement or garage window, but relatively little crime in the area as I well knew. I was drawn to look, curiosity being the most obvious cause of actions, pulling back the curtain slightly so I could see where the vehicles were stopping. They stopped a few doors down and across the street, out of earshot, but within sight of my home.

The sight reminded me of an incident when I was over at my boyfriend's house in my senior year of college. He lived off campus with his parents, and I would often be invited over for dinner with his family.

There, during dinner one night, we saw an ambulance followed by a couple of police cars with their running lights off as they stopped in front of a brick bungalow across the street and a couple of doors down.

I asked Dan's mom if she knew who lived there. She said every once in a while she had seen a young man visit an older couple who lived there, likely a grown son, but other than that, they didn't know them or their names. The older couple kept to themselves, any comings or goings done at a time of day such that they never passed one another. Few people in the city knew all of their neighbors, it seemed.

I went to look out the window as my boyfriend looked up from his dinner with a wry smile and said, "Now don't be a busybody."

I had hoped there hadn't been a heart attack or a bad fall, but no stretcher was taken from the ambulance. The EMT and one of the police officers went to the door, and a middle-aged woman came out. I first thought the woman was giving the first responders some info. I was trying not to be too obvious as I looked out the window, curious as to the actions playing outside the open window.

The woman got into the ambulance with the aid of an EMT and left. The police went into the house, where they remained for some time, and then they too left. I felt silly for looking; it was likely only a small household accident or illness, the police perhaps not even necessary. I wasn't sure what happened, but I felt like it wasn't my business.

It occurred again, the following week, and again, nearly every Friday night I was there for dinner. On the last one, I heard a male shouting. It was very dark when the police left, driving past their living room window, so I didn't know if they had anyone from the house with them. What had been going on in that home was like the moon above; bright and clear white on the surface we could see with nothing but darkness on the other side, no light there but that of the dim gleams that exist on the very edge of endless night.

Finally, a couple of weeks later, we noticed the police and the neighbor woman again. This time, that middle-aged woman was coming back with the police, picking up a couple of boxes of possessions from the young man that we thought was her son, and leaving.

As they did, Dan and I were coming back from a short walk to the library which took us past that neighbor's house. As we crossed the street so that we did not intrude, the older woman gave me an anxious glance, her eyes flat. Then for a moment, her eyes flickered with a glint, such as is seen when you gaze deep into a cistern. What is there that was disturbing that shiny surface; is it something coming to life or perhaps a memory of a monster?

No one had been seen at the house since. The house was not giving up its secrets.

That night I was simply a young woman with that fundamental concern that resides less and less in a world that seems more and more driven to selfies and Instagram, than to normal human interaction. I'm not so naive to know what likely happened in that house. Verbal abuse leads to a slap, to a push, with no visible marks yet, only the fear. There's the returning, because he didn't mean it, he'd had too much to drink; he said it would never happen again. There are apologies, or flowers, or a call to find soberness or treatment. Until next time, when it's stronger, harder, and there are bruises and threats and the cycle starts again. It could happen at any age, to either sex. Men are not immune from abuse, but it's more common when one party is smaller and perceived to be weaker.

I know because I witnessed it at a friend's house as a child, and seeing it, I understand without words in that clangorous chain of remembering. Sometimes they leave, clothes on their back, with their children in tow. Sometimes they come back never expecting that they would die weeping. What remained were only broken lives, and often children cast out to fate, nothing left to remember the one that tried to save them. As the police leave, the flashing blue and red lights gather up every bit of brightness in the darkened world, even as it gets smaller and smaller, until it is gone.

There was no movement at that home in the subsequent weeks; the only light on was in the basement at night. There was no *For Sale* sign; there was no activity. The trees stood watch over something that they couldn't see. I was tempted to walk over, peer in, and see if there was anyone living there, but I stayed away. Some ghosts were best left unsummoned. As a police officer, getting called out on a domestic issue carries with it great risk, and there is often high emotion, drugs, or alcohol involved. Being in a small town doesn't make you immune, so tonight I looked out the window to watch things unfold. I saw a woman coming out of the house holding her wrist, and then I saw the officers talking to an elderly man, waiting along with him as he stood in the doorway in his bathrobe until another younger man showed up. I have met the family. The elderly man has Alzheimer's, and the younger man was his son, probably coming to stay with him while Mrs. Opperman had her wrist checked out by the nearest hospital.

At that point I walked out, waving at my colleagues, who hadn't realized I was at home. They said the woman had fallen and thought she broke her wrist, so they wanted to make sure the son had arrived before they left her husband alone. I understood. I've done a call where I had to administer medicine to a shut-in who had a regular caretaker not show up due to a sudden illness.

This evening made me think back to the situation in Chicago that didn't have so tidy of an ending. I pray I don't get a call on a domestic issue of battery or violation of an order of protection when I'm on patrol by myself, but I am certain the day will come. For now, I'm just glad it was something for which we could render aid.

Chapter 11

———— ✳ ————

Clyde was doing pretty well, having only chewed up one pair of shoes, after which he gave me that doggie look that would seem to say, *well, if you didn't want it chewed up, you shouldn't have left it on the floor.*

I hadn't done anything on the job that would cause me to be injured or fired, though there was one day this week I was worried.

I was on patrol by myself for the first time after assisting the elementary school as an extra crossing guard when classes ended. It didn't take long to cover the whole town. There was Main Street, on which there was the family-owned supermarket. There was the beauty salon, which I'd braved post-academy to find out they had a couple of stylists there that knew all the latest haircuts, not just styles for the grand-mothers. Plus I learned more about what was going on in this town than on any police scanner, as few events or inappro-priate actions were missed by these women, and the informa-tion was always passed around. Note to self, if I'm going to buy wine to take to Evelyn's for dinner, don't buy it in town, I could just hear them now, "Look there's Officer Raines—she bought a bottle of wine *last* year as well."

There was an ice cream place, closed until summer, a tiny chiropractor's office, the bank, the diner, and a little place you could walk in and buy a big piece of pizza by the slice.

There was the liquor store which had never been robbed, and there were the shuttered remnants of the only realtor in town.

The second block of Main Street had the post office, an office of an attorney, another chiropractor's office, and several shuttered small businesses with "for lease" signs in the window. One was a neat and brightly painted business that just had the words "hot dogs" on a sign that looked like it was from the 1970s in that carefully-maintained but long-shuttered building. There are probably some stories there. I'll have to ask Evelyn next time we share a meal.

Between the two sections was the town square. It sat in the middle of a big roundabout which was about as close to gambling as you'd find in this place. Cars come in from six different directions, as the town was laid out almost like a star. You're supposed to yield to the cars already *in* the roundabout but everyone cheats, darting in when there was barely enough room like it was that old retro video game *Frogger*. My mom used to play that silly game, and every time I entered the intersection in the police car, I'd hear the music from it in my head.

That spot had a *lot* of fender benders and resultant tickets for failure to yield. I think I now know why this little town had *two* chiropractors and an attorney.

I'd survived another trip through it, so I headed on down toward the train tracks, near which the only local pub sits. On the other side of the tracks stood our police station and an old railroad station that had been converted into a small museum. That road got a fair bit of traffic as it goes on down south toward the Catholic Church, behind which is a small neighborhood with some families with children. Beyond that, there is a drugstore, a small doctor's office, an auto repair shop, a gas station, and then you're in the open country.

As I got to the four-way stop, looking into the neighborhood, I saw an arm waving and turned to see what was up. There were some children that looked to be young siblings who frantically waved when they saw the police car. This neighborhood had several families with children and just as many dogs. The first time I got a barking dog complaint when out with my training officer, I pulled up to the address in question to find the *only* non-barking dog on the street.

The children were still waving when I came to a stop and got out. I noted no one was injured, but they were pretty worked up about something as their mom watched with concern from the porch.

"Please, please help, our dog got away! The gate was open. We called for him; he always comes if you call, but he must be too far away to hear!"

Just as I'm a sucker for those looks from Clyde; I couldn't ignore the plaintive plea of a child. They were all so cute in their winter gear.

I said, "What's your dog's name?" The oldest little boy said, "Walter."

Walter?

So I did what any other self-respecting law officer would do. I immediately got in the squad car, turned on the lights, and over the speaker called out, "Walter, come here boy! Good dog, Walter. Come here, Walter, good *dog*."

You could probably hear that a mile away.

People started coming out of their houses, laughing at me, but a minute later here came this little white puffball of a dog racing toward the kids. I tipped my hat to them and drove away as soon as all were safely inside their fenced yard.

I understand, now that I've got a dog, how easy it is to get attached. Hopefully, when news of that got back to the station I would not get in trouble for the unusual use of the vehicle's equipment but, as I know how we all are with kids and dogs, I'm sure I would just be teased a little bit.

Chapter 12

———✳———

*Y*ou could see the air mass coming on down from Canada. I couldn't help but think of this one day some years ago wherein the local TV news channel had to substitute a regular reporter for their meteorologist. She appeared to be familiar with being in front of the camera — but regarding weather knowledge — there was none, no matter how hard she tried. What made me snort tea was in her stress in relaying what was on the radar, she blurted out on the air, "From the north comes a giant green blob!" (That would be precipitation, Miss.)

Myself, I relied on Accu-Cow weather for the drive. He's the cow that's perched on top of the diner. No, not a real cow, he's made out of some hard plastic and is life-sized. If Accu-cow was dry, it's nice out, and if he's wet, it's raining. He's always there as I make my way to work or run errands. Today Accu-cow was almost moving in the stiff wind, a wind that was *very* cold.

The icy wind blows down from Canada, Mother Nature pulling the chill deep out of the ground and throwing it in your face, daring you to fight back. It was a frigid mass of air the likes of which I've never seen in my lifetime.

As I look out across a flat horizon, I wonder why this view appears so different than when I lived in the city. Certainly, I could put on a scientist hat and say it was the glaciers that moved down from the north in the Cenozoic era or the giant dust storms that followed that carried the soil away, eventually replaced by layers of volcanic ash from the West, creating a vista of fertility. The difference was more how I live in it, as opposed to its geological origins.

There was something about being able to see so near and so far. Some people feel exposed out in the open land, but I don't. I walked the fields and patrolled the streets, nothing more than a moving lightning rod for those things that might wish to strike me, but they don't. I feel a lot out here in the open heartland, my dog Clyde often by my side, and it was not fear, it was a comfort. It followed me as I walked. The sound of my breath, the whisper of God there in the corn, and the vista of open miles of ground in which I perceived the absolute truth about the past, a truth beyond the buildings and billboards of illusion.

Trees throughout much of the Midwest are few, taken down so that the soil may be tilled, only a few remaining as protection against the marauding wind that cuts through the land late at night like a Viking horde. The cold presses down, pressing deep into layers of topsoil and the bones of invisible deer, who bury themselves further down as if to hide from the wind, creating a stratiform of bones and life and death, forming the coal that is hidden below.

Tonight, this close to the window, I could almost smell the cold, the odor of a whetted knife carving shadows into the night. My body responds with a shiver, and I pull my thick sweater across my chest, tight and warm, and turn away from the glass.

"You ought to move further south," my friends from college would say, "How about California or Florida?" I enjoyed in my youth, like anyone, days snorkeling, blue water dreams, and tropical sun on spring break, but that was not where I wanted to live year-round. I am not at home in such places all of the time, preferring these months of quiet cold. It gives me time to think, to write, to dream broad dreams. The icy fingers down my neck make me shiver, while the fire, as warm as melting marshmallows against my skin, melts me.

The lamplight danced along the walls, my shadow following. Clyde was asleep on the rug, feet in the air, exposing warm fur to a remembered sun of August, feet chasing dusk-colored rabbits within a dream. I think back to tales of my ancestors on my mom's side, who came to the United States and settled in Minnesota. There was a story of my great-grandpa, new to the country, moving a household across miles of land, risking all he had to form a new life out where winters are raw, beating miles of ocean and illness and pain, only to lose most of his money, belongings, and food as wind-swept fire roared through where he lay sleeping one night. My great-grandfather got out, assessed the damage, gathered those small coins he had left to him, and moved on to safer ground.

As I write, the wind sings its siren song against the eaves, daring me to leave, to admit that staying in the Midwest, the land of my ancestors, where I had no family other than my aunt, was not a good idea. I am going to stay. The price that was exacted for learning my way alone out here left my heart an almost empty purse, with just a few scattered coins tinkling in the bottom. I know it was a journey I had to make. You make decisions with what is in the heart at the time, and when the chill wind blows, you take stock of your life and your decisions and seek shelter elsewhere, or you stand and fight for your life and heart and what fuels it. To do otherwise is to wither and die. Out here, the price of innocence is high.

Outside, the wind howls, mute in its anger, with no breath now but a sigh as we make one last trip out to the yard. Clyde and I then flee inside with drumming hearts and warm breath and hoist a challenge to the cold as the fire ignites the night. Down the street, faint windows glow, while the trees outside lay their shadows across my shirt like scraps of black velvet. I close the curtain and pour the wine and listen to my heart.

I pick up a different book tonight: the Bible that had been lying still for so long. In it was the faith of my family, one that I am learning more about each and every day as I look at the world in ways I haven't in years.

They say the Rockies are God's country, but so was this, a small juncture of trees and grass and an old easy chair inside a warm house. This place is a small point in space among a great expanse of glory, where the Trinity is intact because it had never been otherwise, simply tested by the fragility of youth and the passion of yearning. God was lost and then found, postulated here in the open miles of our faith and need.

I think I now understand why my great-grandparents settled here, and I find, more and more, that I am like them. I belong to this cold landscape, surviving like the small creatures outside, by wit and heart and faith in my Lord that has slowly emerged as I continued my talks and prayers with others. As I turn back toward the fire, I listen to the wind, tapping the glass with the resonant sound of a few small coins that are left in my heart, ready to be spent. I think I will start going to church regularly and I am ready to join the others in Bible study. Bit by bit I know that I'm where I need to be, as snow brushes the window like a kiss and I wait for the knock of the wind at my door.

Chapter 13

-------------✳-------------

*T*onight, the town quiet, I tackled one job I'd put off, and that was to sort through my aunt's garage. It was so packed with stuff that I had to park outside. With Clyde safely inside the house and enjoying a nap, I put on a warm coat and went out.

Most of the stuff looked to be boxes of clothing; they were probably my uncle's that I could donate to charity. There's a bunch of Christmas decorative things, a Nativity scene for the yard, lights, a fake tree that was missing most of its needles, and there, something under a big tarp. I removed the tarp to see a flash of red. It was my uncle's Triumph! I remember working with him and my brother on that little British car as a young teen. I have no idea if it runs or how I would go about registering something I inherited and didn't buy, but I was so happy to see it.

My fascination with British cars continued after my teen years on a class trip overseas where I got to drive our host's Range Rover briefly. So many switches to see but fortunately, no matter which one I tried, the same thing happened: nothing. It had all kinds of gauges, most of them there to fill up a hole in the dash, many unlabeled, which would be the automotive equivalent of "door number three!"

I thought for a moment of flipping one labeled "fan." Rumors were a student had done that once and was never seen again. I knew better, getting back to our lodging just as the light faded completely. For a moment I thought I'd light a match to see how much gas I had left before noting most of the back of the vehicle was full of cans of gas (for when the gauge went in one nanosecond from full to empty). I survived that little trip in the Rover wagon, only to come home and find, years later, a British car in my garage.

Once I got the Triumph uncovered and looked through my uncle's written maintenance records, I could see it still needed a new clutch plate, paint, and likely a new battery. New clutch plate? I could do that. No, I could do that after pulling the whole transmission out with some help. I remember when my uncle did the wiring on this car. When you have a British car, it's always time to work on the wiring. I did not do it well, even with him guiding me. My entire wiring experience was watching movies in which some bomb specialist was muttering, "red wire, blue wire," while sweat beaded down their brow while something was ticking.

This automobile ended up as a day vehicle only since my Uncle Frank had figured out that the lights were the "blackout" version that was common during the war, and his car came equipped with them. He tried different things, including the familiar gray shape of rolled welding technology. Once in a while, the brake lights would blink at us like a firefly, but never when the brakes were actually applied.

Oh, but soon all three of us were besotted with bits and pieces of British car all over the shop floor and degreaser in my shower, myself curled up in the lotus position, wedged under the dash muttering "ohm" as my meditative mantra. It wasn't long before I'd heard many things about Mr. Lucas, of British automotive parts fame, especially about him being the inventor of the intermittent windshield wiper. If you've not seen one, it's something to behold. The wiper trembles like a kitten, hesitant to move, when with a sudden leap of faith it flings itself back and forth, movements that soon resemble death throes as it suddenly stops, only to start trembling again when, a couple of minutes later, the process starts over. I got it covered back up this evening as many memories with my uncle and brother came back to me. I hope I can get it running. Maybe my friend David knows something about cars.

So, I'll offer some advice just in case someone ever reads this little online journal. If you can't find one or afford an old British sports car, you too can have the experience. Rent the smallest car you can find and take it out on a completely isolated, uninhabited country road. Turn down the radio so you can hear all the new sounds. Roll down your window, turn off *all* the lights, and start flinging new twenty dollar bills out the window while your passenger flicks a Bic lighter on and off somewhere near the dash as you attempt to maintain centerline at varying high speeds and make sounds that range from "Woo Hoo! Autobahn!" to "is that a hard rubber dog toy in my crankcase?" It comes close.

Chapter 14

———————❋———————

I know it's been a week or so since I made an entry, but between the weather and humans being human, I just wanted to come home and go to sleep.

Evelyn and I did have time for one of our weekly dinners, and I asked her to go to church with me next week. With the forecast being rainy weather, I would be happy to pick her up. I'm glad I have started going back to services again. In college, God became someone I'd call on if I needed to pass a test, not my rock on which I relied every day, in the sunshine and darkness. He forgave me for those years I ignored Him, for which I am grateful, though I still struggled daily with the loss of my family.

I'm still digging through boxes, belongings of my parents when their home was sold that my aunt had put in storage. One of the boxes contained a familiar green sash from my Girl Scouts days.

I did Scouts for several years before Mom got sick. I don't remember a lot of the details besides various projects, a camp or two where I didn't seem to really fit in, and wishing to wander on my own, categorizing the things found in the forest by genus species name rather than joining in to give a wedgie to some kid with braces. I did, however, learn many things, of teamwork, of self-reliance, of myself.

On my honor, I will try:
To serve God and my country,
To help people at all times, and
To live by the Girl Scout Law.

On the sash were my merit badges, the brightly colored bits of cloth that spoke more about learning than that skill for which the badge was given. Looking at that sash, it also brought back some memories of some of what I learned with that banner of cloth. One of the first things I learned was to acquire knowledge before attempting a task, a lesson that has saved my life at least once. Each of those badges represented something new, something viewed with wonder. We did things alone; we did things as a team, which as small children, often meant the tasks were tinged with the innocent absurdity of good intention, even in the face of failure, something our leaders found endearing and not grounds for ridicule.

As I entered my teen years, the acquisition of badges had become, at least in some of our troop, a status symbol, more than an accomplishment. Whoever had the most was apparently winning, though what they actually won was subjective. The quality of the effort was less important than the quantity of the reward. The troop leaders tried to instill a sense of pride in the effort itself, but a few of the scouts were less than nice to those who didn't earn as much bling as they did (many of them had parents who did most of the work for them). "I have more than *you* do," was not merely a boast but a taunt.

Granted, it wasn't all of the kids, just a couple of them, but it was a window into adult behavior that had not changed over time and one that I didn't particularly like.

When our activities became competition instead of adventure, with me getting as caught up in it as the rest of them, I left scouting for other activities that would stretch my mind. Like anyone, I wanted to belong, but I could not do so at the expense of others, learning that lesson for the first time then:

to hold the joy, to contain the peace, and to witness the truth, one must grasp their reward with clean hands.

It's human behavior, though, the need for validation, the same thing I witnessed sitting in the local doctor's office recently. One person states, "I had a double bypass!" to which someone else chimes in, "well, I had a *quadruple* bypass," and so it went, some of the seniors comparing ailments as if whoever had the most artificial stems and valves and joints will win. I could not help but think back to a story of the Christian Desert Fathers who tried to outdo one another in self-mortification so as to die unto oneself, and a monk boasted that, "I'm deader than you!"

We all have those moments when someone says, "Oh I did this, or I did that," and we immediately jump in with our story. I've been as guilty of that as much as anyone, the whole, "been there, done that," probably invented by a type A personality.

Then you had those moments, where what you see and what you witness, were so beyond the pale of anything man could dream up in his personal darkness, that to try and compare was impossible. It's chaos and blood. It's the sound of screaming until the voice was spent, and nothing was left but the ghost of that scream. It's fate, it's history, it's man, machinery, and microbes, and sometimes it's simply a losing battle with physics. It could be a steep slope which you tumbled down in a flurry of words, or it could be a precarious balance, that moment where you came up abruptly to the precipice, only to stop and find you have no speech.

It was at that moment that you understood what faith was made of, its severity, its saving grace, and the power of its secular right to your fidelity.

Sometimes it's the smallest of things, that person on the corner with the sign who may well be a con artist in beggar's clothes, or someone truly sleeping on the streets, their broken bearing sometimes only visible in the eyes, which you would see if yours were not half-averted. It's shouting at the bathroom door that was sticking as it opened, making a sound wood just should *not* make, and then walking outside to see someone's home at the end of the block burned to the ground. It's complaining to a freezer full of food that there's nothing good to eat when elderly people who served their country and worked most of their lives go to bed hungry. It's whining that your welfare check doesn't allow you to have an even bigger TV and a new car, when across the world there are people who know neither Christ nor comfort who sleep on dirt floors, among the vermin and the predators, with no handouts and even less hope, because that's what being poor truly is.

Sometimes it's those big moments. It's getting up before dawn to patrol a silent town, when you'd rather sleep in, to get in a vehicle and transverse miles that might as well be days, to do what you are expected to do. It's standing there under a weeping sky that amplifies what now lies beyond your power to heal; it's accepting that which you have not elected. It's broken skies and broken limbs as if bent by an invisible hand. It's harnessing without hesitation the armored heart that lies within a web of flesh and bone, in which you walk and search and fight the raging fire with little more than your eyes and your mind. It's a holster that contains your responsibility to use that weapon within only as necessary.

There was no badge in the world, Girl Scout or otherwise, that could be granted for this experience and the understanding of what it means. If there were, it would be much like the badge we call Faith. For such times make one more fully aware of just how precious this humanity is we bear, and how easily it is lost (and not just by outside forces). You become aware, and you grow stronger, like lotuses blooming in a fire.

When such a day is over, it's hard to turn the mind off; the visuals are imprinted on the brain, a sudden wheel running downhill, a lantern dashed against the wall, the rending of a sheet of paper. It's hard to get to that quiet place, and when you do, invariably someone asks how your day was. You didn't even want to make eye contact, as you have no words for what your day was, what you have witnessed, how you have hurt, and what you have learned from it. There is little to offer up by way of comparison to any other act of Man, God, or Fate that could go against what one heart could witness.

"So, how was your day?"

I remained silent. If there in my silence, someone wanted to go on about their day, their illness, or money issues, fears, or whatever, I would resist the urge to speak. For to them, in their world, that day, what they were dealing with was as important to them as anything that Fate and Earth can proffer elsewhere. Their fear was not unfounded, for it is their fear, and by their telling, they are seeking hope as well as safety.

Let them have the last word, for there is never enough time to say last words, of our love and desire, of our faith and regret, of our submission or our revolt. To speak them is to shake both Heaven and Earth.

As I drove back from a trip to the city to get my vehicle emissions checked for a new registration, I saw a man in tattered clothing standing at the corner with a cardboard sign under a sky that had lost its vivid hue, fading from blue to a grayish-green, the color of old glass. As I grabbed a bite at our local diner tonight, I looked at the crucifix worn around the neck of the waitress, laying sharp against her skin as she moves, leaving in her wake the scent of spent flowers. I looked to the people around me in my little community, all carrying their own joys and burdens which to them are as real as the bruises that remained on my heart. My journey, however difficult, was no more difficult than theirs, our burdens all of different colors but carrying the same weight.

I raised my head to listen. On this day, perhaps, I could give that much to them.

Chapter 15

--------------- ❋ ---------------

*M*y evenings seem to be reading or chatting with Evelyn or her niece who I got to meet last weekend. I have the little TV, but it might go down to the basement to warn me of tornadoes if I'm down there. I don't watch much TV, as most of what I can get with my antenna is action and crime shows. The majority of them are so removed from actual reality that they are hardly worth watching.

Yes, forensic teams often show up at the crime scene direct from the opera in their $1500 suits, and then stick their faces down into the blood and the gore without even putting on protective masks. Oh, I could go on for days, especially regarding how they'll have DNA evidence in about ten minutes.

Here, in a small town, we have no such teams; if a murder took place here, the state or feds would likely step in to assist, and honestly we'd be happy to have the help. TV is fantasy, what remains of a life cut short is seldom so pretty. If you don't suit up properly, to protect yourself from elements, the terrain, or a hoard of nasty biohazards, you will likely join the deceased on the next table. Then again, there are not too many jobs where you can, on occasion, rappel down a cliff into work.

It's not easy work, and as someone who majored with friends now working such jobs, I understand that we sometimes have to let it out, and watching and making fun of those shows does that for some.

This thought came up when I went for a morning walk and found the bones of a small animal out in the woods. How long had it laid there? Certainly long enough for the bones to bleach to soft white, the flesh now part of the earth, the eyes—empty sockets of history. The shape was benign as if the creature stopped quietly and died, unlike other bones that one finds in the wild, like the animals of the tar pits, trapped in the primordial ooze in the posture of shock. Other animals dropped while running, the bones scattered by predators until the remaining pieces are simply laid out like a discarded jigsaw puzzle.

These bones were in the shape of quiet sleep; as if the animal lay down to wait when death called its name from behind.

It only takes a few days for an animal to decompose now that the weather is getting warmer. I've seen hunters lose their fresh game simply because in the occasional hot temperatures of an Indian summer, a kill left too long can turn quickly. It only takes a few days to return to bone, to the simplest components of life: carbon, oxygen, hydrogen, nitrogen, and sulfur. Only bones are left, pressing into the soft, welcoming earth, the soil a rich bed of late summer.

Sometimes all law enforcement officers find are bones, laid bare to the elements, or burned clean.

With the right temperature, all things will burn, yet bone itself stubbornly resists all but the hottest of fires. Even when all the carbon is burned from it, bone will still retain its shape. An insubstantial ghost of itself, it crumbles easily, the last bastion of the person's being transformed into ash. In that ash remains large pieces, calcined and with the consistency of pumice when held in hand, almost seeming to possess a trace of warmth from within its core.

Even if they cannot speak to us, sometimes what is left gives the forensic technicians a clue. Who was this person?

What manner of violence brought about their end? It's the world few wish to visit, and yet it drives me, the mystery and the puzzle. Perhaps because I realize that the final mystery is within yourself.

The use of physical evidence to build a theoretical model of a given crime or accident scene involves a number of sciences, the chemistry of death, and the engineering of the body. Even in the cold quiet of the woods, I stop and survey the scene, making mental notes in my head. How long had it been laying here? Bones, especially ones that have burned, do not give up a time of death. For that, you need to trace the extent of decomposition in volatile fatty acids, in muscle proteins and amino acids, all which are normally destroyed in a fire.

Even in the woods, simply surveying my environment, my brain sifts through ideas, timelines, and theory based on white bone.

Our department assisted with a fire investigation this year, one that that was intentionally set, for insurance, not to cover up a dead body. I remember waiting as the firefighters valiantly did their work, my skin almost blistering in the heat. Hoping to get close enough to see a clue before it's burned and gone, a timeline of life and death lost to the flame.

Fire doesn't just destroy paper and combustible evidence, it's disruptive to the analysis of bone trauma, especially separating fragmentation patterns resulting from perimortem trauma such as blunt force and projectile impact, and so forth, from those resulting from postmortem heat and fire modification.

Fire suppression, though necessary even if there is no chance of life remaining, also does its damage. The sudden cooling of hose streams may fracture or spall bones that are hot, especially if they've gotten hot to the point of delamination, and it can cause harm that may or may not be salvaged in a laboratory. Then there's mechanical damage, direct hose impact, and falling debris.

The tiny pieces of life's remains that still can speak to us were drowning in water. I stood helplessly by the scene, like a person watching a rescue swimmer who is too late to help, knowing the outcome, yet hoping for something from which I can put the case to rest. I wait, not wanting to turn away, as fire roars right up against the night stars and the deep dark spaces. I wait, while the ice, the silent ice, drips from the trees, melting in the heat of the flame. It is a patient wait, treading carefully on the small broken artifacts of life, part pathology, part engineering, and part going beyond either.

We as yet did not know if a body or bodies were inside, so preserving evidence was crucial. After the mechanics of motion have stopped, after human physiology has broken down, and what once was animated life, a heart that loved, and a soul that dreamed is reduced to flesh or ash, decayed or dried bone, the dead will still bear witness.

They can tell us a story.

It is usually not a story that would make a good television show, and it rarely can be wrapped up in a neat sixty minutes, but it is a story that needs to be told.

Tonight, I write these words downstairs on my laptop as I gaze at a small fire, tended so that it will warm a house surprisingly cold after another front came through. I watch the flames twist and sway in their age-old dance. As humans, we are more than our past, yet we are the same, seeking life and comfort, seeking answers. As I write, gazing at a flame in a fireplace that warms something deep in me, something stirs in memory from the ashes as I go back to my work.

For I realize that, here in the healing walls of this home, my own heart, beaten and darkened by soot, still contains in its core one small piece untouched that may one day smolder back into life, with just the right breath on it.

Life is ice and fire. You can't control what you will feel, who you can save or how they will affect your life. What you can do is take what remains that brings you joy and move forward. It is not the glamorous drama one sees on TV, done for the excitement, the money or the time off to go to the opera. You do this work because you want to, for no other reason. This was a mission that was not assigned, simply a garment of duty one felt compelled to pick off of a bare floor one cold morning.

If another person ever reads my words here, know that the fire burns brightly in you, as it does in me, exposing what is strong and good, what is still useful. You cannot save every heart, but you can save your own heart diligent in its task, even if wounded in battle.

Diligent perhaps, because we've learned through our work that life is precious. We will all die, but we will not all truly live. In doing this, with the small tools we have, with the mind God has given us, we do our part to see that perhaps just one person inherits more than the wind and the dark. In that, no matter hard the duty, I live fuller, breathe deeper, and sleep with peace.

Chapter 16

————————✳————————

Occasionally I have to drive into Oz, as I call the big city of Chicago, which rises out of the cornfields. I go less and less, surprisingly not missing large malls and nightclubs like I did when I arrived in this small town. I'm enjoying just working and coming home to relax in the house, to bake bread with new friends. I may be turning into a younger version of my aunt, and I don't care.

As I made several stops before hitting the freeway home, there were some people panhandling. I have learned to recognize the signs of, "I'm just scamming for money," $300 shoes, smoking cigarettes constantly between green lights (if you can afford a pack-a-day habit, you don't need my cash). There was one young lady, dressed in torn and shabby clothing sporting a *very* recent and intricate hair highlighting job that I know costs close to $200 to get done, even though it looked like she washed her hair with vegetable oil. And look, a new smartphone! Then there was the young man that just looked hungry until you noted how small his pupils are, looking for his next high. Nice try, but they're not getting anything from me. Sometimes I would see someone that had that slightly unhinged look in eyes or actions that made me make sure I avoided eye contact as I ensured my doors were locked, not wishing to put myself in the point blank range of mentally unstable rage.

Once in a while, I saw something in the clear eyes of one of them, noting hands calloused by years of hard work, and realized that whether they were truly homeless or not, they did need something more than cash, an uplifting of the spirit. So on those occasions, I would roll down the window and put out a couple of bucks, but most importantly, I would look them in the eye and treat them with the respect of a kind word and an accepting smile. I remember one of them with tears in his eyes, an older man with a straight back and hands curled by arthritis, simply because I give him a fairly large and crisp bill, called him Sir, and wished him God's blessings for a comfortable night of rest.

Sure, maybe I'm just being played, but I'd rather make the occasional attempt than leave them alone as they sifted through the ghosts of past riches, coming up with empty hands. I've been just one bad decision away from where I had only the clothes on my back and enough gas to make an escape. It can happen to any of us, though I'm thankful I had parents and an aunt and uncle that instilled in me the value of hard work and sweat, never being taught the world owed me something like so many of my peers.

In looking at them, I realize how very precious the smallest of things are, how the most ordinary of things, the simplest of possessions can contain the deep, profound integrity of a work of art. You also realize that you can't hold onto something so hard, so afraid of losing it, that your efforts only fracture what once was whole. I look at some butterflies from Africa under glass that my aunt left in the house when she died. They have such frail and beautiful wings that almost look like they would flutter with life if I softly blew my breath on them. Yet it would only take one accidental drop off the table to destroy them forever, wings tearing from glass that cuts as cleanly as tears.

In our neighborhood, there is this very elderly gentleman, hunched over with pain, barely able to walk. His tidy home on the next block has a wheelchair ramp, for a deceased spouse or himself, I do not know. He walks with great difficulty as if the movement is foreign to him. Each day he takes out his little dog for a walk, likely his only companion as I've never seen him with any family member. Holding a leash in one hand and a cane in another, he passes by, indistinctly and quietly as a shadow, yet with movements that are precise with pain, as his little dog hovers with glee over invisible things in a carpet of grass. When we first passed, and I looked at his face, I expected his countenance to reflect the hampered efforts of a hampered body, pain in his eyes and defeat in his form. Instead, I got a happy glint and a smile as he gazed down at his furry best friend, delighting in just being outside in the warm sunshine with a creature he loved.

Our lives all begin in the same way, in the unleashing of pain as our mothers birth us, in that first deep cry as we take in the air around us. From there, the journeys are as different as our fingerprints, on various paths, some strange, some wonderful, some littered with stones that make us bleed. Some don't survive the journey, others find at its end, they hold a single treasured thing, or nothing at all but their labored breathing. I've learned the hard way that each person, each moment is important.

As I drove into the city today, I saw a woman on a corner in designer business clothing, everything about her bright and shining, but for her eyes. On another was someone in the faded clothes of a working man, which had seen better days, holding a cardboard sign that said, "Need help. God bless." She did everything she could to avoid looking at him, as I handed $5 out the window to him and received an honest and grateful thank-you. I think of what I saw in their eyes—in hers, fear; in his, truth.

Truth, however painful, like beauty, hovers around us, obscured in the still silent waters of a day, waiting for us to stretch out a hand and grab on to it. As I accelerated away, I saw their forms on the sidewalk, joined by others on their way to work, or simply finding their way, looking in the gleaming light like the slats of a fence, some straight, some bent and damaged, all simply trying to hold something together.

Tonight as I type, I look out on my old truck, at a strand of white that's appeared in my strawberry blond hair when I'm barely even thirty, at a scar on my upper chest that marks the time I escaped that opening grave with gentle triumph when a skin cancer was detected early. Others might think it odd that I give money to strangers while driving a nine-year-old vehicle that's seen better days. It has nothing to do with income and all to do with how I can live with myself. Like anyone, I've made mistakes, I've hurt others, and I've known too well those truths that are found in a field where nothing is left but crime scene tape and regret. In those truths is the understanding that none of us are immune from failure, lack of empathy, or fate, but we are still all capable of reaching out a hand to a good soul in need, as Christ did. To be ignored is to disappear, to vanish without provoking either mourning or curiosity, a death in and of itself.

The next time I go out for my walk, I'll take some home-made cookies and share with the old man that walks his dog, I will learn his name, and I will remember it. For he understands too, what many of us know, that no matter how much or how little we have, we all want that same thing—to have a place where we are safe and valued, a place that even the most humble of us deserve to know.

Chapter 17

———————✳———————

*B*eing a police officer was much of what I expected, both good and bad. A lot of the public doesn't like us, and it often involves exceedingly long days, physical discomfort, and, sometimes, danger. Like those who work that brutally difficult and honorable job of firefighter, and those who serve to help the injured as paramedics and the personnel that supports them, you do what you can to get through your day, and that sometimes involves a little well-placed humor in quiet places.

It had been a long day, a bad car crash with injuries that required us to stand outside in the elements and reroute traffic away from the town square. That was followed by a report of an abandoned baby that turned out to be a doll a child had left sitting against a lamp post. Then there were the sore muscles from attempting to climb a tree to get someone's cat down (yes, I went to college for four years for that). So everyone was a little on edge.

Then a call came in about a horse that had gotten loose. We just cover the city itself; the rural areas are covered by the sheriff or the state police, but this was right at the edge of town, and the last thing we needed was *My Friend Flicka* running through town on the same night the pub had a two-for-one special. We alerted the sheriff just to be sure, so he could send a deputy out in addition to our officer.

The call had come in right at dusk, a complaint and a possible danger to the public in this dark, flat land. Having busted out of its stall perhaps, "a pony running free in the roadway."

I couldn't resist—as I called the dispatcher on my phone, I said, "I'll pay you five dollars to get on the radio and say the pony's name is Wildfire."

It wasn't five seconds later, "Complainant advises pony's name is Wildfire."

You could almost hear the laughter across the county, and the diligent young man that was sent out to investigate does not put it together. I wouldn't have either if not for my mom listening to 70s music a lot.

On scene, he's even confirming with the owners of the horse that had, "busted down its stall," that the name was, indeed, Wildfire, so that he could accurately note it in the report. Word is the middle-aged owners just looked at him like he was perhaps a bit strange. It wasn't until he had closed out the call and was back at headquarters asking, "What did it matter what its name was?"

Insert sound of hand slapping forehead here.

When I got home, I picked up a book I was reading about the exploration of the North and South Poles. Until the early twentieth century, both the North and South Poles remained alluring unknowns shrouded in a biting cold mystery that demanded resolution. Only a century ago, intrepid men dreamed of conquering the planet's last continent with tools unfit for the purpose. For those men, heroism alone sufficed.

It's not easy being a leader. I'm a rookie, yet in the community people look to me for direction, knowing it's my job to keep the community engaged and safe. It's not always easy. It takes patience and humor, as well as knowing what battles are worth fighting.

People, I have found, are vastly complex, with many facets that never show until placed in a certain light. We all place such a value on nothing more than face value, quick assumptions of a person's character, by what little snippets they show of themselves. You have to spend time with a person, face conflict or danger next to them, to see what they are made of. You can't rely on what you hear, certainly in politics, so much of the media spinning its version of the truth. It's easy to get caught up in such situations, making judgments based on what's in the news, what's trending in social media. If I've learned anything, it is that in any situation involving people, it's best to step back and reserve judgment, for that which you see for yourself with your own eyes. Anything else is as fragile as glass and elusive as smoke.

So in reading that book tonight about leadership and courage pushed to the limits in the worst of conditions, those things that leave their mark, that haunt the edges of our almost understanding, I thought hard about coping with such adventures. I've been there, but not even close to this level on my worst of days.

The author did a fine job in exploring the fraternity that experienced not only heartbreaking defeat, but even death; those who have gone to the absolute edge of no return and had the choice to either continue, to find the land they sought, or hurtle over the world's screaming edge. It was a land of little mercy. Salomon August Andrée and his Arctic balloon never returned; Ernest Shackleton called it quits only ninety-seven miles from the elusive South Pole, and his countryman Captain Robert F. Scott succeeded, only to cruelly perish returning to base.

With his death pending, Captain Scott wrote, "We are weak, writing is difficult but for my own sake I do not regret this journey, which has shown that Englishmen can endure hardships, help one another, and meet death with as great a fortitude as ever in the past. Had we lived, I should have had a tale to tell of the hardihood, endurance, and courage of my companions which would have stirred the heart of every man, these rough notes and our dead bodies must tell the tale."

Articulate grace in the face of death. Daring to even begin the journey. Such are the things that drive the courageous, the visionaries. Those who earn their names know what risk is, and they take up its burden anyway. They pursue, without ambivalence, one bright shining goal, be it an exploration of a new land, or the promotion of an ideal that should be heard. Walking headlong into the deepening shadow of the unknown, they hold aloft a hidden flame and sacrifice what is familiar for what is unknown. Such is the nature of valor.

When Captain Robert Scott's returning Arctic party was down to three surviving men, they were hit by a final blizzard, a ceaseless, battling roar of a storm that made further travel impossible. Almost out of food, water, and heat, they hunkered down in hopes of an impossible rescue. When there was no heat left, only some mentholated spirits, Captain Scott devised a makeshift lamp with a small piece of lamp wick, so that in the dim light he could continue to write. There was no food left or water, and he was holding on for the sake of his men. He made one final entry and tucked his diary into a small green canvas pouch and gently nestled it underneath his head as he lay down to sleep that long dark sleep of yesterday's omission and regrets, the tent answering only to the howling wind.

His last scribed words, "Final Entry. For God's sake, look after our people."

We are but one act of nature, one mistake of humanity from being in a place echoed in the brave words of Captain Scott. A place where, by some failure of eye or hand, the ranting of a terrorist state, the involuntary flick of the atmosphere, or simply geography, we are faced with death. There, by fate or human action as remote to indictment as judgment, suddenly too close and too late, you are there. Rushing toward that final crescendo, hoping that providence and momentum won't spew you out the other side before you have one last chance to turn the wheel to get your ship and crew to safety.

All I ask is that when I die, I still believe strongly in what I cannot help but believe and what I cannot help but be.

I have people who rely on me, whose well-being I am bound to protect. I would only hope that if I ever faced that sort of situation, be it tomorrow or years from now, that I could show such strength. That I could stand stalwart in the hopes that they might live, inextricable from the scattered remains of courage that blow through the infinite passages we seek.

But if we can laugh a little along the way, even better.

Chapter 18

———————※———————

I finally met the man from whose home the violin music came. He had recently moved here, the cost of living in a rural area allowing him to start his own business. He works from a shop behind his home where he lives with his wife. He looked *so* familiar to me, and I couldn't figure out why until he mentioned a cousin coming to visit. His cousin was my geeky friend David from college! That explains the resemblance. I told him when his cousin came to town, let me know, and I'd have the three of them over for dinner.

David and I were still good friends, but we had both been so busy we'd not talked as much. Though he and I took a lot of science classes together, he changed his major to computer science, finding he had a gift for designing computer programs. He is still up in Chicago, likely working from home on his computer, developing things I couldn't run without adult supervision. Computers aren't my strength, but I have so enjoyed making these entries every few nights. He has started on what will be a great career and that he can do it from home most of the time is even better.

It would be fun to see him again. My old boyfriend hadn't even sent a Christmas card. He was the one who wanted something less serious, but I was hoping we could remain friends. Apparently not. I still heard from some of my city friends, though not as often. Evelyn's niece Jan and I had taken an outing to Chicago one warm, sunny weekend, so I had one friend my age. Evelyn also mentioned an elderly gentleman that I'd seen out on walks, not the one with the dog, but the one that always wears a hat, no matter what the weather. She said his name was Harry, and he had no family. He loved books, but his eyesight wasn't good enough to read; he would love it if I could come over some evening and read to him. I totally get it about not having family and told her I would do that.

Being the only female currently working for the police department as an officer, the previous one having retired, I'm careful in the community to set a good example. I avoid the town's only pub except to eat lunch with one of the other officers, though Evelyn and I will sometimes have a little glass of wine with dinner at my house. Being an officer in a small town is different from the urban environment. We know the citizens here, and they know our families and us. In the city the respect might be given to the uniform, but here it is given to the individual. That respect must be earned. So I'm sensitive to how I dress and act, just as I am sensitive to the fears and concerns of the people who share this community with me. I'm careful about where I go and ensure that how I speak is a credit to the department and my church family.

I'm becoming more comfortable here, less bored and less wanting to head to Chicago to meet up with people that want to do more partying than living. There is no movie theater; there is no Starbucks. The only grocery store has a pickle barrel, an old-fashioned butcher and a collection of freshly baked goods every day. The hardware store is off the square in a little shop, and the manager seems to have forgiven me for giving him a ticket, though there has been no further mention of a date. I like the place. No matter what you need, you can simply state it, and the owner somehow, out of all the rows and racks of things, knows exactly where it is. After the hardware store, I'll stop in at the little Italian place with no tables, only a counter where you can walk in and walk out with a slice of homemade pizza as big as a hat, made by the owner's grandmother. Then you can eat it, or one of their Italian ices, as you wander off the square by the little library, into one of the older neighborhoods, exploring the heart of this place. The ancient mapmakers would put on unexplored regions, "there be dragons," but on the quiet edge of town spaces, there were only the watchful eyes of a gargoyle that holds his breath. There's an old, old church, a small graveyard behind; an angel holding a book in her hand, a Bible perhaps, or just a book with a single line that says, "There be ghosts." I move away in hushed silence, treading softly on the hard, patient earth. A few blocks away is the pub, on the wall of which is a wooden woman that once graced the bow of a clipper ship. Now she watches out the window for the train that stops outside that might be bringing her an errant sailor.

No one has huge houses or lots, and the neighbors know who you are, even if their houses aren't feet away. Some keep to themselves for the most part, but they all watch your back. They know when you're gone so they'll come over and shovel your driveway, so it looks like you're home, a chocolate cake making its way back by way of thanks. Most of the houses have big porches. At night, now that spring is here, when everyone is home from work, we'll gather to barbecue in our driveways. Then I will sit out on my wide porch, as an iced tea is tipped to a neighbor passing, looking through the branched intervals overhead, as the finishing of light fades from the zenith of the darkening skies.

This is a working-class town, and just as we know the satisfaction of taking care of our own, we relish those times we can just sit back. It's a small place that most city dwellers would pass by, turning up their gourmet noses at the diner that has a cow on its roof (but we climb on up there and put a pretty scarf on him for the Easter season). It's a place where churches are packed on the weekends with more retired farmers and military men and their families than you'd ever meet elsewhere. This is a town where men came home from four years away from family and decent food; fighting for that hard, patient ground that could wait, assured it would eventually claim them, fighting so they could return with that gravitational pull to the place they were born, to raise a family and eventually rest in that ground that was home.

What I have here is not fancy, but it is becoming beautiful to me, it is becoming my truth. These are not words I use trivially, that by so doing, so easily deprives them of not just their force, but their dignity. What I have here, what is contained in these walls, is not just antique books and old tools, but that which lives and breathes, that I wish to keep.

Chapter 19

———— ✳ ————

I think the cold weather is behind us; Evelyn thought as she brought some things in from the car. Harry waved at her from his window. She was glad he was in such good health for being in his nineties. He had enjoyed Rachel reading to him a couple of evenings a week. In turn, he taught her how to play dominoes and cribbage, games that her video-game generation had never experienced.

She was glad Rachel and her niece Jan got along well, but Jan was busy planning her wedding, so she didn't have a lot of time to socialize.

As the moon first knocks at the window, she pulls a loaf of bread from the oven to cool as she looks for a container to put the rest of the stew in the slow cooker away. She had eaten earlier and was enjoying the stillness of the house.

Outside, the world is quiet, the four walls around her corralling her in, even as she is free to leave. There is still much to do, clothes fresh from being washed and dried to be hung up, the remnants of her baking to be tidied up. On the floor, her old Lab twitches in her sleep, swimming against the impending night.

Outside, somewhere far in the distance, a coyote howls. Evelyn looks out into the darkness, into the ancient and inscrutable face of the night, seeing nothing, knowing that doesn't mean there isn't anything there. The light is faded, the wind brisk, the flow of the outside lights, small incandescent intervals of safety around the house, challenging anyone to come near.

She finishes her chores, turns on some music, and sits by the front window, the lights off and the curtains open, so she can keep her eye on her world. She's not afraid of the dark, not with her husband's Colt and her courage, a mother bear that will defend to the death her home and her life. Behind her, a small lamp stammers its light; the shadows tossed upon land on which glaciers once slowly roared. From a distance she can hear the sonorous waves of sound from the woods behind her home, floating out to her, the cry of an owl, and the howl of a predator. The sound builds, merging with the sounds inside the house, a soft laugh of remembrance, a bit of a song, a resonance both subdued and rich, rising and retreating like a harmonic tide.

In a vase, a single flower, small and delicate, watered by hand, carries its scent into the home. Water is plentiful here, but in some parts of the world, it is as rare and precious as love. When it falls, it falls in huge drops that seep into bare skin, wetting the formerly barren ground, soaking in deep with the weight of an astonishing gift.

She looks delicate, but she is not, having seen both the drops of water and drops of blood that fall on the foreheads of the innocent. She is not unaware of the dangers that being a woman alone can pose, predators seeking defenseless prey, even in small, quiet towns.

That is why she is concerned to see Rachel's truck home but no lights on in the house. She understands she's strong and a police officer, but what if someone was to lie in wait for her?

She grabs the Colt to put in her pocket and goes over, not noting anything unusual; however, the door isn't locked.

"Rachel, it's Evelyn; are you OK?"

From the back of the house comes a familiar voice, "I just forgot the door."

Poor thing, Evelyn thinks, *she sounds like she has a cold.* From the back of the house, there is a light, there in the kitchen. On the table is a bunch of family photos through which Rachel gently sifts through as tears softly fall.

"I'm so sorry Rachel," was all Evelyn could manage before Rachel flung herself into her arms as if she were her small child, sobbing and saying, "Why did God take my whole family?"

There, those words, that was the doubt and the pain that had this poor young woman turn away from a Spirit-filled life to one that had little direction. How long had she been keeping this locked up inside, afraid to fully open her heart up, unable to fully heal?

As Rachel continued to cry, Evelyn looked up with a start to see a form in the door—it was Miriam's husband, Ezekiel, the neighbor with the violin.

"Come on in," Evelyn said, "she's just had a rough day."

As he entered the light of the kitchen, Evelyn saw he wasn't Ezekiel from down the street. He was younger, probably Rachel's age, but had the same eyes and hair color as Ezekiel. "I'm sorry for interrupting—I'm David—Ezekiel's cousin and Rachel's friend."

At the sound of his voice, Rachel looked up. "I'm so sorry you are seeing me so messed up right now, I just really missed my family today, and it hit me all at once when I sorted these pictures."

David gently sat down at the table while Evelyn went and got her a tissue.

David looked at Rachel and gently said, "I heard what you said. God didn't take your family to punish you or to hurt you. I can't tell you why they all died so young; only God can answer that, and I bet if you asked to talk to your minister in private, he could give you words far better than your favorite IT guy."

He paused for a moment and then continued, "But what I can tell you is this. Think back to when your parents decided to have children. They had to know that there was always the possibility that those children would know pain of some sort in their lives, or that they might well unintentionally cause you grief. They still had you because they knew that as you grew and learned you had so much potential for incredible times of happiness and great love. God knew when you were born on this earth, as His child, there was no guarantee you would not ever suffer, but you would know great joys and find the wonder in life. Your family is safe now in the Kingdom of God, and I know you will see them again."

Rachel sniffed and nodded, as she gently touched one of the photos." You're right, and I think I will go talk to the pastor about it. I'm sorry, Evelyn. I know I shouldn't have been bitter about it. Thanks for helping me heal."

Evelyn could only nod and watch this young man with her; something told her he might have had a little spiritual push today to be here and it was clear he adored Rachel.

"Well, David, if your cousin wouldn't mind, how about you and Rachel come on over to my house as I doubt either of you have eaten. I have a big batch of stew that is still warm and homemade bread, and I think if we asked real nice, Harry would come over and play a game of dominoes with us."

David looked up and said, "What are dominoes?" To that, Rachel replied, "Oh, you city slickers don't know anything!" And she laughed through her tears.

Chapter 20

———————✳———————

K *eep it, or throw it out?*
Cleaning out the closet and drawers as winter clothing is cleaned and tucked away in storage, deciding what to keep and what to give or throw away is sometimes not an easy decision. Some items are worth mending, but only if there is enough wear left to make it worth the time and effort. Some items that look like someone lost a jousting match with a can of paint are easier to toss away. I was tired from doing the clean-up and happily came upstairs to update my journal.

Most of us regularly go through our things, to clear space, to create room for new things, sometimes to the point where it's almost an obsession. I've met people that cannot function if they don't shop almost daily, often for things they don't need and can't afford, just because they have a psychological need to buy something. I once was sent on a wellness check with another officer to a home that belonged to a hoarder. There was barely any light, but for the lamps, items piled up over window height; a gloom that brooded over the clutter, as if angered by the light that came only with the flip of a switch. A single person lived there, with no room for family, for visitors, only for more possessions, most of which were in bags never opened.

I found that unbearably sad; even more so than the reason I was there.

In some ways, all of us are prone to gather up things that take up space. I certainly have more lathe bits around than are likely allowed by law, and my aunt had pots and pans of every conceivable size in the kitchen. There are also copies of cooking magazines, and many books, but those are things we use and re-read.

I remember standing outside one night at a fatal motor-cycle-crash scene, finding sense in the senseless, finding my purpose even as sparrows fall to earth. People watching from a distance would think me too quiet, too still; shouldn't this activity be a frenzy of lights and motion, like on TV? I have found that there is much activity in being the quiet observer, standing in a stillness that smells of silence, breathing in so many scents in the cold, damp air. Sweat, blood, and a flower that only blooms in the dark, the wind so scant it's like breath on a mirror. Each smell blended yet distinct, always overlaid with the copper tang of life spilled. The air hummed along to the night's quiet as all I see, smell, and feel, forms into a sub-stance I can almost feel on my flesh, capturing it, recording it there in the stillness. The truth was often still, inarticulate, not knowing it is the truth.

I knew then what my reality was, and it was not trading up my aunt's home for a much bigger one full of things. Our reality is held only by us, not by others. They can only see the show, never really knowing what they are truly seeing.

Now my house is tiny, warm, and full of the abandoned and reclaimed, some of the wooden furniture rescued from a curb and restored. So much history here, so much laughter as that work was done, once with my friend David helping when he was visiting. I look at it now, not with that quick glance that is a short day, greedily grabbed and then forgotten, but in the sustained light of memories made.

It was a busy weekend of "spring cleaning" mostly involving the garage so I could get at the Triumph. There were also bags of trash and non-repairable clothing and such out in the garbage bin. The sun was setting, the sky and the horizon welded in one bright spark, soon to be snuffed out. Everything around me dissolved into that last bit of warmth, bags of trash, heavy in my arms, everything in them at one time, fashioned out of love, duty, or desire, which all bear their own weights.

One of the things I found that gave me pause as I cleaned was an apron of my mom's that was left here one Thanksgiving. But that will be a story for tomorrow night.

Chapter 21

———————✳︎———————

*D*ear Journal: I've never written about it before, I'm just now learning about how to talk about such things. Mom was diagnosed with Alzheimer's in her fifties. Since my dad didn't have the best heart in the world, the two of them had long-term care insurance. It covered assisting living and nursing home care, but Dad steadfastly refused to put her in a home, caring for her at home, even in his declining years with my helping as I could.

Initially, she had her little moments of forgetfulness, like any person her age, but she was such a bundle of energy, still active in church and volunteering, taking dance classes, working in the garden. Then one morning, out of the blue, she came into the kitchen and sat down, looked at me and I realized *she did not have a clue as to who I was.*

What struck me was not that but the look on her face as she realized this, realized she *should* know. I obviously wasn't a bugler or a neighbor over for coffee, I was a girl with red hair like everyone else in the family, wearing a fuzzy robe that she had washed and put in my closet the night before. I will never forget the look of her at that moment. It was the most starkly exposed face I'd ever seen, a face in which unknown terrors haunted the edges; the face of a fledgling dove about to tumble from the nest.

It came into our lives quickly, one moment she was laughing, engaging in board games and puns with us, her face bright, and her wit, razor sharp. Then came those moments where everything just went sort of dim. The doctor only confirmed what Dad had suspected and kept from me for some months until he knew for sure. *Alzheimer's*. It's a terrible disease for all involved. We read what we could about it, we planned as a family, and we prayed. There wasn't more we could do.

As the next two years passed, there were a few moments she was quite lucid and happy. Those moments were the hardest for all of us. In those brief minutes, she was fully aware that her mind was going, what was happening to her and how helpless she was to do anything about it.

The disease's progression was as predictable as its course was certain. Mood swings and aggression, words that made no sense, dropping to the floor like marbles, tears as she tried to mentally gather them up, anger at the very air around her. She always was gentle with my dad, though. Only with him would she remain calm, the reasoning that was blind and deaf somehow responding to something in him that her mind could still see.

Dad cared for her patiently, no matter how bad it got. Friends couldn't visit, for they were strangers to her, and she'd go into a furious rage if anyone but us tried to enter the home. Dad was her calm and her constant. I was able to help with the housework and the cooking, but he refused to let anyone else care for "his girl" or to send her to skilled nursing care. When she passed, it was quite sudden, after she contracted pneumonia. From her sudden coughing to her collapse, it was just days.

Sometimes when you get to the far edge, the edge just breaks away.

We laid her to rest on a tree-covered hilltop in a little cemetery. My brother and my dad are on either side of her. I visit; I bring flowers. Sometimes Evelyn goes with me, and we hug and shed some tears, neither of us immune to having our hearts broken. Then we smile through the tears, sharing our stories as we make the long trip home to photos and a small stuffed bear that Mom had sewn.

One of those photos is one of her and Dad on their first date, and you could see something in their smiles that would be lost on so many people. Not many people could have cared for her by themselves as my dad did, for so long, but I understand. Love is a story that tells itself.

On my couch is the form of a little black dog. I do not know why Clyde was a stray. He responds with great plaintive urgency to the sound of small children laughing, looking around for them as to say "my kids, my kids," only to get this look of pure sadness when he sees they are strangers. The first time I witnessed it, I cried.

I was so happy to get him, a saving grace in a house that had a gaping hole in it. What we hold close to us and what we let go is as telling as the words we say. It took me years to understand it, but the words of Henry David Thoreau make perfect sense to me now.

"The price of anything is the amount of life you exchange for it."

I realized that there were certain things, and in the past even certain people, that simply violated my sense of thrift, exacting things out of me well beyond their worth. That concept was lost to me when I was a teen, but as I got older, with truth stripped of its cloak of immortality, it was clear.

As I take out some things to be picked up by a charitable group, I look around me. Shadows move like ghosts over the sun, deepening the grass to the color of jewels. The snow is long gone, the dark earth trembling to release spring's flowers. At the side of the house is an old trellis that needs repair work before new life grabs onto it yet again. I gather it close to my chest to take it inside to be mended, rather than tossed away. This is my home; I think as I bend my face down to it, breathing in the scent of old wood, holding the weight securely as I move inside. I could bury my face in it, this small thing to be salvaged from this place that I had always been seeking.

As I type these final words tonight, all I can think is that hope and love, love and desire, can be what propels us silently onward. Hope and love, love and desire, can also be merely sound that people who have never hoped or loved or desired have for what they never possessed and will not until they forget the words.

Chapter 22

———————✳———————

*W*ell, dear Journal, I've been neglecting you again. There was a lot going on in our community during and following the Christmas season. Last December, I got to participate in my first burglary case by watching one of the officers who is training me, and we had more than our share of people imbibing too much of the holidays' spirits, but overall it was pretty quiet.

With the holiday season long past and some rainy weather still lingering on, I have time to catch up. There hasn't been much in the way of children playing up and down the block. A healthy dose of rain topped with a late spring snow likely meant that any Christmas gifted bikes or skateboards would have to wait until sunnier days.

There's only one family with young children on our street. Most of the residents are empty-nesters, the newly-weds looking for more modern dwellings closer to the trendy neighborhoods in bigger cities, rather than this quiet street dotted with mission-style bungalows and the occasional large brick home of bygone eras. I do enjoy watching the Garcia family's four children play, the youngest still with training wheels on his bike, always tended to by his mother or his oldest sibling. Their father is the second generation in this area, taking over management of one of the larger businesses in town.

I imagined them on this last Christmas morning, that day of cheer, peace, and the setting aside of grievances for goodwill. There would have been the sounds of the children squealing as they opened up their new toys, with paper and ribbon flying. As a child, I was no different. Evelyn put a Christmas stocking up with my name on it near her fireplace so that I could find an orange, some dark chocolate, and some lovely hair ribbons in it on Christmas morning when I picked her up to go to Christmas service. I think she realized that I'm very much a little kid at heart.

When I was a child, the focus of Christmas was Christ, not the presents, but my mom and dad made sure we had a few fun things to open up after church, as well as the stocking. My brother was quite a few years older than me, but he was always good about letting me play with him, even if I didn't know what I was doing. I remembered back to one Christmas afternoon as we ran little toy cars up and down the hall, bunching up Mom's carpet runner on the hardwood to make hills and valleys for his little white toy Mustang to careen over. There were kid-sized tools, and games, and imagination. I was never big into video games, but he had a few, and I'd watch, fascinated by all the sounds and colors.

He'd even let me play outside with his older friends, though I could not yet throw a ball or swing a bat well enough to be a part of the team. I appreciated his acceptance. So many days we spent just riding our bikes through our big city suburban neighborhood playing soldier or policeman. It didn't matter what names or faces we called ourselves as long as youth coursed through us, that immortal brief moment in life, all possibilities held within our minds and loss was but a shadow in a distant room.

Somewhere, for most of us, that changes. Toys give way to clothes, to books for school, to the practical, to the necessary, if we're lucky enough to have a family to get a gift from at all. If we're fortunate, occasionally we have friends and family that go out of their way to find the unique, that which serves a purpose, even if that was simply a big smile.

Where did the years go? I know I'm still considered quite young, but thirty is getting closer. I wonder if I'll ever marry and have kids of my own to wreak havoc on my carpeting. Evelyn told me I'd have a husband if it were God's plan for me and to be patient.

It's taken some time, but with the help of my pastor and my church family, I'm learning to let go of the past, of anger and acrimony, the unabsolved and the unforgotten. As I met like-minded people and made new friends who lived for wonder, not drama, my first Christmas in this town became a precious time, a quiet time. It became not just a time of gifts but of giving, of laughter, and gestures and love measured out like medicine by a loving hand. It has been a long journey, of love lost and found, but it's one that brought me here, to a small hundred-year-old bungalow, filled with old tools and antiques, a collection of books and furniture, some of which was found on a curb with the trash and lovingly restored. What often was deemed worthless by one person was another's treasure, and each time I see my reflection in a well-polished surface, I am reminded of that.

Chapter 23

————————— ✳ —————————

*G*ood evening, Journal. Yes, it's been a few days since I made an entry, but there was a lot going on. I spent the morning with Sergeant Beazly, my field training officer (FTO). He's not the only FTO I would have these first months as a police officer, but he would be my first as well as my final one. He's been great, even letting me drive the squad car during my first month last fall. Some of my classmates at the Police Academy that I've kept in contact with said they were still riding "shotgun," not having been allowed to drive yet, but they are in bigger cities with a lot more to watch and observe. Sgt. Beazly and the others have taught me a lot, even as I discovered there are things I should know how to do in a small town department that I don't, like how to change out a toner cartridge in the copy machine. Seriously, that was harder than field-stripping my weapon!

Every task, from a stop, to arrest, to an investigation, to patrol, I've observed them do, often more than once. I would observe and make mental notes each time before I would be allowed to do it myself, still under their supervision. Even though we are a small department, we use a training model known as the "San Jose Model," with three four-week phases during this last fall and winter, each on a different shift and under a different FTO. Now I'm getting into the fourth phase with Sgt. Beazly, my original FTO. This phase of training would be the "shadow," or "ghost," phase. In these upcoming two weeks, he will be going with me in plain clothes, with me in uniform. He's only along to be an active observer unless something goes south quickly. He's simply there to watch and document. And they document everything. So far, the only solitary things I've done are more community-related, like helping direct traffic or children near the school or following an accident where I'll do a quick patrol around town on the way back to the station. I would not be sent out alone to any calls. If I was to see something on one of these patrols, coming back from the school or town square, I was to call for backup.

During those times on my own, I've learned to really watch people and notice how poorly they pay attention to what's going on around them. My generation and those behind us are the worst, constantly distracted by their phones or other electronic devices.

On our last drive to the town south of here where there was a hospital that my FTO and I needed to visit to interview a witness following a vehicular accident, I saw a young woman in stylish dark clothing with a cap pulled down over her forehead in the chill, with her head down texting. Obvious to the danger, she was walking in a turn lane of a busy four lane intersection, only a couple of feet from the heavy traffic, barely visible in the early morning gloom.

Elsewhere, each and every hour a teen is hit by a car and injured or killed by texting and walking. I think I need to ask one of the training officers if there was local statute or code that we can use to charge someone for just being a complete idiot.

The more I viewed the world around me and others' apparent lack of understanding that man and nature wish to kill you when you're not paying attention, I am continually amazed, and not in a good way. Just Google "Bison Selfie" for a lesson in that.

Knowing when to stop, knowing when to press on, and simply knowing where you *are,* seem like such simple tasks. Such decisions aren't just daily ones; they can be the ones on which your life may one day depend, as I'm finding out very quickly.

When I was still a teen, I once walked along a forest trail high up in the mountains on a hike with a high school friend and the cousins she was visiting in Colorado. As I smelled the wind that carried on it the brisk deceit of fall, promising moments of golden warmth, I didn't think of the sudden storms that could deliver six inches of snow that no one had planned on. I was only a teen, learning the rules, learning myself, eager to get away from adult supervision and the smog of civilization.

Even as sunlight flirted with my face, I looked up into clouds amassing as if for a conference and heard the rumbling that was the portent of plummeting expectations for the promised golden day. I wasn't sure whether I should continue to climb up on my own, as I had forged on ahead of the others into darkening foliage, or head back down below. There were times, with experience; you could derive the truth out of the complex and troubled heart of the wilderness. In such moments you know with your own heart, already bruised, that it's time to listen to your instincts. I did so and headed back down a familiar trail while there was still ample light.

Though I've only had to deal with three dead bodies so far on the job, and one was a cow (don't ask), I realize that our fate was just a quick flicker of asphalt and blue that could swallow you in an instant, before you're even aware that it is happening. It's not something you can ignore, head down reading your latest text or email; it's LIFE. It's risk, and it's motion, life swirling around us, seeping in and under each window and door that you walked through, barely slowed by the camera click that is time, those irrevocable moments that were your glory or your demise.

113

Sometimes I've seen it in town, the collision between an old Saturn and a Smart Car, the ambulance having driven away, thankfully only a broken nose and back pain to address. I have found that what remained was telling, the cars having shed their skins, bits of fiberglass and plastic strewn about, the rest of the vehicles' remains removed in a bucket, so to speak. Sometimes I saw it out in the country in my vehicle, snow drifts that looked so serene; waves tossed up against farm fences, but other signs told of the dangers that had been here, two cars still in ditches and the one jackknifed semi in the median.

We will learn our capabilities if this town ever suffers a natural disaster. Despite modern medicine and a lifestyle that allows most of us to live well into our 80s, take away the power, the phone, the trappings of modern life, and something ancient can stir in the dark hours. Not that we will feel helpless, but there will be a subliminal awareness of something among us, something lurking and dark, that lies low and quiet, pulling itself up by sharp claws to the edge of our world, looking at us as prey.

My grandfather went to war, not for months, for but years, witnessing things no man should see and coming home only to find that the world was so changed, that his old self, seemed to have no place it in it any longer. He found life and friends among the deceived and dispossessed that returned, each with their scars, playing cards at the lodge, hoisting a beer and reaffirming that although they were now old, they were still on guard, on watch, until the final taps would be played.

As with any law enforcement officer, from rookie to seasoned, I've seen the aftermath of what comes from being unaware of what was happening. It was a copper taste of blood and fear that took more than a shower and a pint of ice cream to put to rest at the end of the day. Fate and poor choice, when wed, have no end to their appetite, and are reluctant even to throw out a bone for the labors of those who pick up the pieces.

I view each day as a gift. I'm not owed a good one, or even another one. As I got home tonight, I looked at the landscape as I entered the house, the golden haze of the sun shimmering upon the drive, waiting for the first refraction of darkness as the night moved in again. Here hovered my world, watched over by my God, a daily journey, and lesson as I divided humankind's intent from its actions, even as He divided the light from the darkness. I gave quiet thanks for this day, hoping for another.

As I make this journal entry, a young woman walks by the front of the house with a tiny dog on a leash, eyes half closed and head bobbing to the music playing in her earbuds, oblivious to anything outside of her sphere as night closes around her small form. As she passed, I heard an internal "click" in my head, that moment of time, fixed here forever in a picture that only played against my eyelids. May she continue in safety, is all I could think.

How old is fear? How is it acquired? And when do we start listening to it? Something was running through me that defied prediction. Outside in the night, coyotes gather at the edge of darkness, rabbits run away as a trusting young woman walks into the shadows.

It's time to put such gloomy thoughts aside and go to bed. My training officer Sgt. Beazly and I have to serve an eviction notice early tomorrow at that run-down rental house at the south edge of town.

It's time to turn off the computer and pass into the night.

Chapter 24

———— ✳ ————

*E*velyn wakes to the sound of birds outside her window. It had been a restless night for some reason, and she is aware of a sense of unease she normally doesn't have. As the rumble of thunder creeps in on the horizon, she looks out toward the trees, to the chattering of birds as she steps outside to let Boo-Boo the retriever out into the yard to do her morning business.

On the ground are two doves. When the old dog approaches them, they scoot across the ground rather than fly away, their brains not sensing the danger. Fortunately, the dog shows no interest in them. Above the doves, two cardinals flutter like two tiny flags among the branches and then fly away, as if the wind dispersed them like small scraps of cloth. On the railing is a small sparrow, looking a little worse for wear, staring at the empty feeder, watching her carefully, wondering if she will harm or help. On the air, the echo of all of their cries melds together in a melody that is mournful and plaintive, barely able to be heard above the wind.

She thinks of the Bible verse, *"Look at the birds of the air: they neither sow nor reap nor gather into barns, and yet your heavenly Father feeds them. Are you not of more value than they?"*

She looks at her refrigerator as she goes inside; on it is a thank-you note Rachel wrote her for a little gift Evelyn had made for her: a cover for her Bible, now that she is attending Bible study regularly. She is aware that Rachel is still sometimes struggling with her faith, her world torn apart when she was still just a teen, an act that pulled her away from her path to God. That is why she continues to talk with her and pray with her as she hopes that Rachel will soon see how very loved and blessed she is.

Evelyn is still not certain why she feels as she does this morning. Maybe it was a bit of Rachel's mood as they chatted briefly before bed on the telephone. She too was very introspective and more pensive than normal. Perhaps that's just because of the intensity of her training right now. She urges Boo-Boo back into the house with the promise of a treat, the old dog not straying, keeping to the yard unless given the command to do otherwise. As she looks around the yard, she finds the still small form of a mouse. Whether it was a raccoon or a housecat, something had laid a mortal blow to it, probably frightened off before it could finish its meal as she let the dog out. She carefully watches the woods until Boo-Boo is safely back in the house before she gently gathers it up and buries it deep out in the back garden, the ground still hard from the cold.

Like the rabbit and fox, the small creatures of the cold and the sometimes desolate fields, Evelyn remains alert, holding on to her faith and her life as best she can, looking out into the darkness that is the deep woods at this hour, always aware. For she has lived too many years on the planet to know that evil doesn't just come with blazing light and trumpet. It comes in swift secrecy, clothed in the illusion of peace, disregarding the law, full of intent, coming to us quietly, draped in the cold, dark garment of winter that falls to the ground with the ease of dew turning to morning frost.

Breakfast is made, and dishes washed, her dog gently snoozing on her bed, as she dresses and gets her car warmed up, needing to go to the small feed store just outside town to the south for bird seed and dog food. Soon it will be warm enough for the birds not to need her help, but she knows they may still have a frost or two in the forecast before Easter.

As she nears the edge of the city limits, she finds herself a block behind a police car. She wonders if it is Rachel and the officer who is training her. Last night as they talked on the phone, Rachel had mentioned something about having to perform a task in this part of town first thing in the morning.

Evelyn slows for a suicidal squirrel to allow it to get out of the road when she notices the police car stopped at a house that's right at the edge of town. It's a place that she never lingered near when out on past walks. It has overgrown empty lots on each side and looked to be in a state of disrepair. Perhaps the person here is just elderly and can't do the upkeep. She'll ask at church to see if there's something someone can do, a work party perhaps.

The house is set back about thirty yards from the street. A front window is open, but the curtains were drawn, which makes the porch appear even darker. Almost everyone in town, it seems, has a porch, and on any given summer evening, there's usually someone sitting out, even if it's the teenager down the street with the streak in her hair dyed bright blue, hanging out with her young friends. On those summer nights, if you listen carefully through an opening in the double-paned windows that are so very, many years old, you might hear the music of the neighborhood, the sounds of things that go back to our roots, our families' roots, even as society changes. This porch, though, looks like a "no trespassing sign" come alive, with all matter of junk blocking the front door, which is likely never used.

She slows to a crawl as she sees the door open on the stopped police car as the road is narrow. Yes, it is Rachel, and she waves, but Rachel doesn't see her as she gets out of the driver's side and then walks to the passenger side to speak to her training officer as he exits the car. Evelyn is about fifty yards away with her car when, just as Rachel walks toward the front of the vehicle from the passenger's side, her training officer standing behind her, there is a loud popping sound.

Evelyn thinks, "Is that firecrackers? What idiot is firing off firecrackers this time of the year?"

The noise is not firecrackers. It is a sound that cleaves the air, the sharp dry report, the abrupt wild thunder of untamed horses, and the whispering smoke of one's fate.

Rachel goes down, blood soaking her shirt.

Chapter 25

———✳———

*E*velyn thinks this has been the longest day of her life since her husband died. One minute she's getting ready to honk and wave and the next moment she sees the young woman she's come to think of as a daughter lying on the ground bleeding as another shot pings off the top of the police car. Rachel's training officer had hit the ground on that first shot and quickly pulled Rachel's body further back behind the vehicle by her feet.

She jams on her brakes and dives down to the floorboards once the engine is off, wanting to get out and help, knowing she could likely be killed, something that the training officer would have to carry with him his whole life. She can call 9-1-1. It's only minutes when it seems practically every police officer in town is here, there's noise and shouting through a megaphone but fortunately no further gunfire.

She wishes she is any place but here. She tries to picture herself in the little town park with Rachel and Boo-Boo and Clyde, taking the time just to sit, the dogs hoping they were under a dog biscuit tree. There we would wait, serene and still, the moon shining on nibbled shadow, content to just sit underneath the starry sigh of heaven. The only other lights would be as far off and distant. They would not dwell on shame or pride or loss, barely remembered like the smell of decay, sensed only in the instant of its knowledge and then fading to dim memory as you move away from it, dark and far away, as such things should remain for as long as possible.

Evelyn is aware that all there is now is noise, which is ever so adept at replacing hope. She tries to think of happier sounds. The sound of her mother's voice comes to mind. She struggles to remember her voice as she died more than a decade ago. She does remember her smell, a mixture of clean rain and Chanel No. 5. It's a scent, like that of sandalwood, that Evelyn can't catch a whiff of now without going soft and quiet, with this little echo in her chest.

Evelyn's dad kept a few of her mom's things around after she passed such as her light blue sweater that she left draped over the armchair where she would read in the evenings. He also kept her pink bathrobe; the one Mom wore in her last days in hospice. Evelyn claimed them both so she could smell her scent. It was as if their presence somehow compelled her home to remain, more than brick and mortar, but the place that held the essence and character of the woman who often graced it. However, with the passing of time, just looking at them in the silence was simply an affirmation of emptiness, and soon, they too were put away.

She still has them tucked away in her home, the sweater and the robe, but she does wish she could remember her mom's voice. One of her earliest memories of hearing comes from the waves of the ocean, there on the shores of South Carolina where they visited her dad's sister one summer vacation, a sound that flirted up against the sand while she played with a little bucket and shovel while gulls cried around them like mewing kittens. This aunt was a lot older than her dad and passed shortly after that, but she can still remember that trip and those sounds. She remembers so many sounds as she grew up. There was the clatter of her mom juggling pots and pans making them dinner every night, and the spray of the garden hose as her father washed their car every Saturday. She recalls the wind pouring through the trees, and later, the sound of a bugle at her husband's funeral, the last sound she ever heard that made her feel as alone as she is right now.

Evelyn known she has something else; she has the power of prayer, and she's going to pray as hard as she's ever prayed for anything right now. Crouched down in her vehicle, she bows her head.

It seemed like only minutes had gone by when there is a sharp, soft sound at her window.

Tap. Tap. Tap.

"What is that sound?" she thinks

"Mrs. Ahlgren, are you OK?" Evelyn recognizes the voice. It's Eric Jacobs. Just a few years before, he had been one of her students, recently joining the police force after several years in the military. She keeps up with a lot of her former students' successes after they graduated. Not having kids of her own, she took pride in how she taught them, trying to set a good example of character when she was a teacher.

She looks up and says, "I'm fine, but please, how is Rachel?" Her voice cracks with the words.

He looks at her with care and says, "She should be OK. The bullet grazed her upper arm. There's a lot of blood vessels there, so it looks worse than it is. The tissue damage isn't bad, but she's in shock. They're taking her to the hospital in Brownstown with her training officer, who was uninjured but didn't want to leave her side. She wanted to come over and check on you, but they insisted she go to the hospital as she lost a bit of blood."

"Thank you, Lord," is all Evelyn can get out, even as she still has so many questions.

"How did this happen?"

The officer replies, "I can't tell you much right now, but there was a large meth lab in the home. The shooter saw the police car, not knowing they were just serving eviction papers and panicked, probably high on drugs. He was out the back door before we got here, but we'll catch him, there's lots of evidence, and he panicked and left on foot since the police car was blocking the driveway, forgetting his phone and wallet in the process."

Two hours later, Evelyn is at the county hospital, as Rachel holds her hand from her bed, pale as a ghost, but warm to the touch, a large dressing on her shoulder. Outside, one of her colleagues not actively working the case hovered, still concerned for her well-being as the other officers search for the suspect.

Not knowing if the suspect is still armed had everyone on edge, but the officers would do their best to get him safely behind bars. A fleeing suspect is less of a threat than an approaching one, but if he is on drugs, the unpredictable behavior involved with that has to be factored in. Rachel had been trained, like the other officers, that they were only justified in shooting a fleeing suspect in a particular set of circumstances. The 1985 Supreme Court case Tennessee v. Garner having narrowed the so-called Fleeing Felon Rule, which previously held that law enforcement officers could use deadly force on a fleeing person suspected of a felony. Now, officers can only shoot a fleeing suspect when they firmly believe that the suspect will cause death or serious injury to the officer, other officers, or the public, if not apprehended.

Rachel says a quick prayer for the safety of her colleagues, as she gives Evelyn a reassuring smile, knowing she must look like a mess. She knows her face has quite a few scratches on it from being suddenly pulled back from her prone position near the front of the vehicle by her FTO as he tried to get her behind cover. That action likely saved her life as although she hit the ground when she heard the shot and the pain in her arm exploded, she was still partially exposed.

Evelyn looks at her gently and says, "Rachel—when you get home I'll make a honey-and-herb salve for your face for the scratches."

Rachel responds with a laugh, "Mom, quit fussing over me."

"Mom? Do you have a head injury too?" But Evelyn smiles.

Rachel smiles back at her, preparing to speak. "Yes, if it's OK, you can be my unofficial mom from now on if you don't think that's disrespectful to my mom's memory."

Evelyn squeezed her hand back and said, "I think your mom would be pleased that you are happy, and I would be proud to be your unofficial mom."

She wasn't going to stay long. They were going to keep Rachel overnight, just as a precaution, but outside of blood loss and a furrow that required some careful cleaning and some stitches, she would recover fully, though she'd be off work for a bit to allow the wound to heal. Fortunately, there was no deep tissue, nerve damage, or bone injury and it was her non-dominant arm. She was one very lucky young woman. She was also someone who had a very busy Guardian Angel this day.

Rachel looks at her as if she knows what she is thinking and squeezes her hand.

"God is good," they both say at the same time and smile.

Chapter 26

———————✳———————

Well, my Journal friend, it's been a while, hasn't it? I'll be back to active training soon when my stitches come out. I'm going to have to do some strength training with that arm. Keeping it still as it healed certainly didn't help my muscle tone. The man who shot me was apprehended and with a previous conviction for arson; he won't be out of prison soon. He was trying to hitchhike south of town after running through a few miles of farmland when the State Police picked him up without fuss. Fortunately, he was too tired from fleeing and in too poor of a physical state to put up much of a fight.

I was beyond angry with him at first; how he could care so little for another human being to take their life over some drugs—for that was what he intended to do. That wasn't a warning shot; he was aiming for my head or heart. After seeing him in court and the damage that meth had done to him, ravaging his face and body so that at thirty-six he looked seventy years old, I could only pity him and pray for him.

My FTO still felt awful about what happened, having no idea we were walking into an ambush. No one has ever been so bold as to make meth within city limits, but as more and more people become addicted or make and distribute the drug for profit, it could happen again. We are going to have a city meeting with those who hold rental properties, suggesting they write the ability to inspect a home as part of the rental agreement. We hope that might deter someone with drug trade or use in mind from renting within city limits. We're also going to hold a series of community meetings to talk with our residents about the increasing dangers of drug activity in rural areas, what to watch for, and the importance of alerting us if they see something going on. Brookdale is typically a pretty quiet town. If they notice unusual comings and goings, loud noises late at night, or frequent fights among occupants or visitors, we need to know so we can keep them safe.

Looking back on that day, it's all a blur, but one thing stands out in my mind. I was not seriously injured or killed, because I turned to the right and back, just as the trigger was pulled. Instead of a direct hit, the bullet grazed me on the upper left arm instead of hitting me in the chest which it would have if I'd moved ninety degrees left, to pass in front of the squad car from the passenger side.

Why did I move the opposite direction of where I needed to go?

I heard my name called out from behind me.

Sgt. Beazly said he didn't hear it but thought it was likely Evelyn calling out a greeting from behind us in her car. But I know Evelyn's voice, and it was not her.

I remembered Sunday service after I got out of the hospital; the Communion pouring chalice glinting like a newly minted coin, surrounded by people that treated me like family, as from above, the bloodied and life-sized Christ crowned with thorns looked down on us with kind eyes that had seen too much. I watched His face, smooth and impenetrable, as I took a sip of wine from my little cup. As I swallowed, I took in the blood that contained an indomitable spirit which came from the fire that exists in us all, looking up at Jesus there on the cross with a conspiratorial nod and silent thanks, having no other words.

All I can say is, I am forever blessed to be here still.

I can't help but think back to my grandfather, who came under fire in World War II. When he went overseas, there was a good chance he would not come back; millions were killed in that war. Grandpa never imagined that he would not come back; he never told himself that he and Grandma, already engaged, would not be married, would not have children, and would not make a life. Even in times of great battle, he held the final prize in his hand, never doubting that it would come to be.

He watched over that dream as our Father in Heaven watches over us; His creation shaped out of the primal absolute that contained nothing and all, knowing we are equally as capable of being ruined as being saved but believing we will be saved, as to believe anything else is to perish.

We all have our dreams, just as we all have our fears. I think of my friend David's Cousin Ezekiel, the man down the street that plays the violin for weddings at our church with an incredible gift, having been taught by his blue-eyed mother whom he misses so much. As a teen, he was offered a scholarship to study music at a University in the southern part of the state. He turned it down; his passion was creating, inventing things out of form and void and wood and noise, things that touch his brain and his heart—for what the heart holds becomes our only truth. People come from a hundred miles away to buy his handcrafted furniture now, made there in a shop behind their tidy home, where he and his wife are so happy.

I talked to my grandpa every night before he passed, there in his dwindling days. He had done a lot of which he could be proud. He had been an accountant, a deacon at the church, active in his local Lion's Club, as well as a husband and a father. I asked him if he had any regrets, things he wished he had done. I asked, not to remind him of regrets, but to see what in his mind's eye was important, looking back through so many years.

He said he had no regrets, but when I asked him what he was most happy for, his answer surprised me. But then I understood what it meant.

Grandpa was married twice. His first wife, my Grandma Helen, had died in her sleep just shy of her sixty-fifth birthday. It was her heart they said. He grieved but eventually remarried a kind and lovely widow who took on his grandchildren like they were her own. We all thought the world of her, and he genuinely loved her. After she too had passed, as he neared his end days, it was the photos of his first wife that came out of drawers and sat on the table by his bed. So I was at first taken aback when he said, "I'm glad I loved and lost Helen."

He said that not because he was the one that physically remained after she died, but because he was glad that he had followed his heart, not his good sense, which meant not asking her to marry him and wait for years because he might not come back. Because if he had not, she would not have become the one he had to grieve over because he chose to abandon the idea of them when he went off to war.

I know it's not likely anyone will ever read this journal. If some day they do, I'm going to add these words: Dear reader, I'm going to tell you something. As you look around your life this day, think about things you'd like to hold onto— flesh and blood, wood or glass, paper or plastic. Do not think about all you will risk to get it. Do not think about how long it might take, or even if it will be what you expected. Do not ask if others will like it but only that it will bring beauty into your life.

I looked at the photo of my grandparents when they married right after Grandpa got back from Europe that is on the shelf next to my aunt's old desk. They look both innocent and immortal, even as they look slightly amazed to be saying those vows.

I look at the things in my office, one a beautiful chest, what they would have called a "hope chest" back in Grandma's day. It was built by Ezekiel and purchased and placed here to be filled with things Evelyn has crafted for me such as a beautiful bed covering, and some lacy things for the table and home. With it are a few things that belonged to my mom that I kept with me through the years. All of those items are objects that print the often silent mold of our dreams and desires, as easy to be ignored as small fairy feet, when they are magic indeed.

People ask me if I'm going to quit being a police officer because of what happened. I am not, because when I close my eyes it is still my dream, and I can make it real.

Chapter 27

———— ✳ ————

I was back to work this morning at an hour and temperature that denied not only sanity but breath as our town had received one last cold snap before spring was officially over. Sgt. Beazly was going to assign another FTO to go out with me, but I told him I wanted it to be him. What happened to me was in no way his fault and with the investigation over with, we had no need to talk about it further.

Given the array of community-service tasks we do as a small-town police department that in larger cities would be handled by other social agencies, as well as a public perception that small and rural areas are mostly crime free, leads some to believe that policing in such places is quite safe. In truth, our work can be demanding and dangerous, and I won't be the first small-town cop shot this year, just hopefully, not for a long while.

Outside of the initial wake-up hour, I enjoyed doing patrols early in the morning with my FTO. With fewer cars on the road, it gave me time to ask questions. It also gave me time to think, to reflect back upon those might-have-beens that are truer than truth. Outside there's both beauty and abandonment, a few miles of old neighborhoods and darkened buildings, interspersed with areas of renewal where some young people would buy the old abandoned houses for a fraction of city pricing, to fix them up and become commuters.

One thing I noticed as we drove was the light, not from the sun, as it's an hour from tipping its hand, but from the street-lights, as they shone and reflected on window and form. I saw bits of light in the few other cars that were out, making a long drive to a job in Chicago. I'd notice the glow of a cigarette, a dome light that comes on and then off again as someone changed the radio channel or took a drink of coffee before going back into dark hiding as quick as a trap door spider.

As we drove, words flowed through my head, some which might splay across a keyboard one night, others that although they gleamed like lit from a candle within, would only burn in the darkness of my thoughts. As Sgt. Beazly drove and I sipped coffee to stay awake, I found myself lulled into a cadence where I'm remembering while aware, as the squad car moved around a known chunk missing in that street, as a hand in a body still dreaming, flicks away from a cold candle, with the heated remembrance of pain.

I realized we were not here to daydream, and even though thoughts flowed through my head, I'm looking in great detail at everything around me, looking for something out of place, something amiss.

I did the same thing when I lived in the city, working as an intern one summer before graduation at one of the local crime labs. As I drove to work during that time, I remembered how the light flicked off the glasses-adorned face of someone waiting for the bus. Their form was tired; their head down as if with grief, with eyes that had forgotten how to weep, but remembered well the tracks those tears left on their skin. They'd be out there in warmth and in driving rain. On such mornings, I drew my rain jacket around myself, thankful for the blessing of my vehicle, so I didn't have to wait out in the elements for transportation.

More often than not, the forms waiting for the bus were female, going into the city to work, often the only one working in that household. In this poorer part of the city that I would pass each morning, too many homes lacked a father, and the women did what they could to keep family and home together. And so they would wait for the bus as if waiting for the light, not for the glare of victory but only that which they needed to see to endure. As a child, I never would have pictured myself moving to the country, always vowing to live my whole life in the city, where the crimes I'd uncover would be like all the crime shows I grew up watching, exciting and mysterious. My most recent call was going with my FTO to investigate a domestic complaint. The husband and wife admitted they had argued loudly with a window open. The woman said there was no threat or violence just a boisterous disagreement regarding her mother. We mediated the conflict and left with the determination that the husband would stay in the family room without dessert until he said he was sorry. That and the occasional stray cat turned in was more my day than in the inner city.

I also thought the city was more exciting, constantly in motion with all of the people bustling about to activities, to a family. No, unlike Brookdale, the small town I lived in now, the city was as open as the eternal springtime of a young woman's heart, and it was full of sight and sound and motion. With life comes change, some full of wonder, some that are nothing more than cold forceps tearing free some of that which is familiar. Now, to my surprise, that place, that big city, no longer seemed familiar. It was in my little town that I found the quiet warmth that was a familiar heart.

Up ahead were flashing lights, an early morning train. I didn't know how many times I've watched someone drive around the lowered gates, as they risked all just to gain three minutes of time, making that dash as a distracted night bird does as it dove into the fatal glow of a window. Up ahead by one of the city buildings, the school bus was quietly parked waiting with the patience that only something that is surrounded by children can truly understand. When I patrolled in the afternoons, I would see that familiar and square yellow form, young girls inside waving their curls and their cell phones, taking selfies as young men hover nearby, wanting to be noticed, waiting for those moments when a girl's heart senses something more than self.

"Don't grow up too fast," I said to those young women who may find it too easy to give themselves up at the first mention of love when the person uttering the word has no idea what it is. I am glad I waited. Despite my partying and some occasional underage alcohol consumption, I had been firm in my wish to save myself for marriage, likely a key factor in Dan breaking up with me.

As the school bus turned and moved away, more and more lights dotted the road ahead of us, as the diner opened its doors, and more cars entered the roadway. The movements and the light triggered more memories, the light being the substance of remembrance itself, the sight, sense, and self that the brain recalls long after the muscle memories of the moments were stilled.

As we drove, stopping to check on a small business that had an interior light on too early, only to find it locked and quietly vacant, I thought about my house now, dark but for the kitchen light, the dog waiting for either Evelyn or Ezekiel to walk him. I did the same for their pets, feeding them and walking them if they are out of town visiting family. I missed my friend Jan, Evelyn's niece. The friendship remained even though with her new marriage, she didn't have so much free time.

My stomach gently growled as I took another sip of coffee. There's no rule about it, but I chose not to eat in the squad car. It was not due to any aversion to crumbs but rather, not wanting to do a self-Heimlich on the steering wheel patrolling alone if I took a bite out of a donut at the same time I saw another completely misaligned bumper sticker for someone that should be in jail, not politics. Our meal break of the day was coming soon; we'd stop in at the diner to buy a meal, something the owners appreciated, thanking us with the free coffee they also gave the senior citizens every day.

As the sun comes fully up, we drove along the edge of town, farm fields in the distance. Over them were low clouds, distant white masses, coiled as if convoluted in form, not appearing to move, yet somehow changing, their journey as much of a slow discovery as mine.

Up ahead was the flashing light by the school. I don't miss the big-city driving. There were too many clogged freeways. Many of them had lights that flashed to let you merge onto an already overcrowded road, one vehicle at a time, a color that struck as if sound, the deliberate hammer blow that you think would be the last but were repeated and resumed, long after the last vehicle was past hearing.

One thing about driving here and there was the same. Each and every set of headlights holds a life, one no different than mine but for its past and its future, each of us God's children on a journey, as we stirred and murmured on this moving watch that was a morning commute or a small town patrol. Some were listening to music; some were only looking at the world around them with a broad yet distracted listening. Each and every one of us continues to make these small journeys, taking from them something new each day.

Chapter 28

———————— ✳ ————————

*T*o my Journal: I understand I pretty much ignored you all summer, but I helped Evelyn with her garden and with learning how to use her laptop. We also did a bunch of canning, so we have veggies this winter. I've learned to love our little local grocery even though it doesn't have the selection you see in the city. However, it has an in-house butcher, and all of the meat is prepared locally, including their home-made sausage. I no longer giggle at the giant pickle barrel because it sits right next to the table where all of the in-store baked Polish pastries are, the original owners being immigrants who moved out here years ago to start the business their children now run. The store has everything I need and sometimes Evelyn and I would shop together, getting the giant bag of potatoes or a large family pack of meat and then splitting it up, so we wasted neither money nor time.

I'm continuing to read to Harry a couple of nights a week. There's church and Bible study, and David is visiting more often and helping me get my uncle's Triumph running, which has involved many weekends. I also think that I've learned the layout of this town well, though I still chuckle when I hear locals refer to the small section of houses built after 1968 as "the rich part of town."

Summer is finally over, and I have exciting news.

I am finally off of probation. Though none of the other officers ever called me "rookie" I was well aware I was one. Contrary to what some of my old friends thought, there's a lot that goes into becoming a peace officer. It's not like you get your degree or the work and life experience you need for this and someone hands you a badge and a firearm and says, "Go on out there and fight crime." My whole first year was learning, and unlike big city police departments, we handled a lot of other activities that are normally done by other social service agencies, which had a learning curve of their own.

Everything I did was performed at least once by another officer while I observed and usually twice before I did it while being scrutinized. If it were something more complex like a DUI, I'd watch several times. That first year I was never truly alone but for a couple of times that I directed kids or cars when school let out and could take the car there my own. Even the time I busted a teen with a borrowed drivers' license trying to buy liquor, my FTO was outside within earshot checking out damage next door that was reported to be vandalism but turned out to be a nearsighted bird and plate glass.

I had the good fortune to talk to some police officers before I made this career decision, and they gave me some good advice. I tried to follow it, and I tried to keep my ego in check simply because I had a degree from a big-city University. What these officers often had in the place of that was military experience, something a lot harder than college, something that made them grow up while I was still acting like an idiot hanging out with those as immature as I was.

I had learned that being a know-it-all was no more popular here than when you were in third grade. There were many times I kept silent when I knew the answer, finding that by not speaking, I learned more than I already did. Our Chief belonged to my church, and it was good that he ran the department based on Christian values, even if he didn't directly address them as such. Treating each other as we wished to be treated ourselves kept morale up, and though forgiveness didn't apply to state and local law, we could forgive the individual in our hearts. More than once I got home and in my nightly prayers asked for safety for the person who I had given yet another speeding ticket to, hoping they would slow down before they got hurt or harmed another.

I didn't make too many errors that first year though my FTO still ribs me about the time we pulled over a young man, and I was about ready to make an arrest as he smelled very much like a skunk, which is also the fragrance of very low-grade marijuana. He insisted he was clean, at which point my FTO pointed to the side of the road where there was a very flat, yet odiferous skunk. I felt a little sheepish, but the young man took no offense and was happy to take the warning for a license tag that had expired the previous month, promising to take care of it now that he was home from college and was using his car again.

Today was the first time I did patrol duty all by myself, as opposed to a quick patrol coming back from school. As I drove, the radio came to life as the dispatcher reported an erratic driver coming off of Sherman onto Maple headed north. That was only a block away from where I was, so I got going.

I spotted the car described up ahead. Although the car in question seemed to be driving OK, I turned on my lights just as he entered the dreaded roundabout around the town square. I sounded the siren so others would let me in behind him. But rather than veer onto one of the six streets that hub off of the roundabout, with all the cars coming out of businesses on those side streets making an exit as treacherous as the entry, he just kept going around and around in circles. With no place to pull his car over, I gave chase at 15 mph. On the fifth circuit around the circle, I looked over near the grocery store where there was an officer directing kids across the street, and he's doubled over laughing.

137

I got on the speaker. "It's clear at the bank, exit there and pull over, I'm getting dizzy."

I expected either a very young driver or an elderly one. The driver was in his sixties, well dressed, and didn't appear to be under the influence. So I couldn't explain erratic driving. Then I looked down and saw a bag from the gas station snack aisle and two scratch-off lottery tickets on the seat.

"You were driving and scratching!" I exclaimed.

Sheepishly, he admitted he was. He had no prior traffic issues on record, so after checking back with the station, I gave him back his license and released him with a warning about distracted driving. I also told him that next time I pulled him over for such an occurrence, his winning ticket would be from me, not the State of Illinois.

So, dear Journal, it's been a learning curve. Anyone who has ever watched that TV cop or forensic show thinks every call is going to be some high-speed, high-action incident, which we will solve in one hour with the outcomes as clear-cut as night and day. It's not like that. We certainly have crime. As drug use in rural areas picked up so did petty theft and burglary in town. Dealing with a belligerent drunk was never fun. Neither was entering a dark building not knowing if you will find a rogue opossum or someone much bigger than you on drugs, looking to steal something.

It was less like what was on TV and more like securing an open utility box that someone called in or showing up with the fire department to deal with the smoke alarm that was the result of someone's failed attempt to broil a steak after too much Chardonnay. In some ways, I viewed it as more policing than big-time law enforcement. We were there, at all hours of the day and night, in the sunshine and bitter cold, providing protection and presence so that the residents know that our intent was to keep them as safe as we could, sometimes risking our lives to do so. There were law-abiding people in town that owned firearms to protect their homes, lives, and property, something I certainly understood. We were just a few individuals, and we couldn't be everywhere at once, and finding that out when someone just kicked in your front door with intent to harm you wasn't ideal. So we do what we can and knowing the men that I worked with; I think each of us would give our all.

The mainstream media often misrepresents police work, giving attention to only the rare bad officer and not the thousands of good ones. That makes the citizens' expectations of us so different than what they should be. That is why I'm glad I live in a community where most of the residents know my name and respect me for trying, even if they are going to tease me at the diner about my little car chase today.

Chapter 29

———— ❊ ————

I am very thankful to be safely home tonight after a long drive. It's hard to believe it's been more than two years since I started this journal. I realize I haven't made an entry in a year, and the Christmas holiday is approaching yet again. It's not like life has been boring. I'm off probation, have mastered the copy machine, and Evelyn is trying to teach me how to knit. I've met all of my neighbors, and I've made friends with a couple of the younger wives in the neighborhood. I even found a used bookstore in the next little town over. Crime has been low, though we had a rash of burglaries of vacant homes—the thieves entering through basement windows. I now have a bolt that goes from my door down into the floor frame in the sunroom where the basement stairs are.

Burglars may break into the basement, but they are not getting into the house that way.

Fortunately, the suspects were apprehended, and they turned out to be a couple of career juvenile delinquents from Brownstown, now old enough to face charges as adults. We also had a vehicle stolen from the grocery store after someone left it running with the doors unlocked. Wherever you live, that's not a good idea.

Today, the miles hummed beneath my truck, as I made one last trip to Chicago before the worst of winter to have coffee with David and attend the wedding of a former classmate. I was anxious to get back to my house, back to the little town that was now not a temporary resting place but my true home. I did not have the radio on; my eyes were outside, taking it all in, the weather, the dangers of the road for the unwary, there, underneath the steady whisper of tires, the strong, purring power of the engine.

Suddenly, I heard the sound of metal being molded into a shape it was not intended for, punctuated by a simultaneous horn. At the intersection ahead of me, two cars had collided, not violently by any means, but with enough force to cause damage to both vehicles. A car with numerous dents and expired plates had failed to yield to a larger vehicle. Doors were flung open and the young, unkempt driver of the car who failed to yield, started yelling at the other driver, cursing him that it was his fault with an onslaught of profanity that would make a sailor blush.

The driver with the right of way was in his early 60s, I'd say, with a ball cap with the name of a military unit on it. He stood calmly and firmly, suffering the words of the younger man until the police showed up to sort things out. I admired his calm, but I doubt it's the first time that outrage was directed at him by someone for simply doing what he was expected and charged with doing. One of the officers got out of his vehicle to direct us around the wreck as quickly and safely as he could. I noted the area we were in, planning on making a call to the local police department when I got home, letting them know they had a witness if they needed one.

There were cars stopped ahead of me and behind me as we waited for the damaged vehicles to be cleared, or at least a safe path made around them until the intersection could be reopened. Between my truck and those two dented vehicles there was a small and beaten-up older car. The young lady in it opened her window and started throwing several days' worth of empty bags of fast food out the window into the street, the round "Go Green" sticker on the back of her car nothing more than a big blind eye to the litter she was leaving for others to clean up.

Behind me was a lady in a van, the windows streaked with sunlight. I saw some movement in the back of the vehicle and thought that she must be a soccer mom. First I heard the bark of a dog. Then I saw a few little heads pop up behind her as I looked in my rearview mirror. Not soccer, Scouts, I thought, as I noted the neat haircut and a little uniform as one of them opened the window to look out as far as he could since we were at a full stop. That made me smile as I remembered my early days of scouting, the learning of self-reliance, good citizenship, and respect. I thanked God that there are still those who instill those teachings in our children along with the families that support and foster those qualities.

Due to some road construction, after I had cleared the accident area, my route took me through the central part of the city, not a really bad part, but one I wouldn't want to walk alone through. On a corner stood a young woman, makeup applied with a trowel, shivering in a short furry coat which barely covered cheap tight clothes, her thighs straining what little fabric was there. The fabric was bright pink and written across her backside, in shiny rhinestones no less, was the word "LOVE" in big glittering letters. I guess I'm reading the wrong fashion magazines; my pants are khaki and just have pockets for a money clip and a comb.

She's not waiting for a bus and was likely a prostitute, but given the blustery wind and spitting snow, no one was stopping for her. As I waited for yet another light to change, a man stopped his car by her and rolled the window down. Was it a customer or someone asking for directions? It was neither.

No, that was probably her pimp. The expression on their faces was obvious, hers, the high flush of shame, his, one of ownership and anger. I whispered, "Please don't get in the car." She doesn't, she shouted something at him and walked away. As she passed me, I rolled down my window and as she came over I quietly handed her a card. On it was the name of a group that one of David's friends works at, one that helps the victims of vice and abuse. She looked at it and quietly said, "Thank you, honey," as she sauntered off. I wish I could have done more for her. There were always those who preyed on the weak, offering up what appeared to be shelter and sustenance, not for any altruistic means but only to take from them what was needed to retain control.

As I drove through the streets of increasing urban blight I couldn't help but notice a society held together with paint and words; both intended to hide the sight of baseless delusion. Doors were shuttered from neglect, even as men sat idle like a rusty tool in a workless hand while others scurried to their labors like ants, bearing the burden of those who did nothing.

I wanted to get through here before dark. Because in the night, animals in human form roamed with unlawful tooth and claw, while honest men and women traveled too often in fear, moving hurriedly through a dark vacuum in which no help may come, as the night air trembled with the shuddering sound of silent drums.

Just a few miles further and the blight turned into expensive apartments and condos, rising from the depths of the city. Some were new; some were restored; the young flocking to upscale parts of the city. Some were the Spartan apartments of working University students; others were condominiums that cost more than some farmhouses on large chunks of land. In them lived man stacked up upon man, small spaces filled with shiny trappings of want, yet likely only provisions for a few days. Turn on the tap and water flowed, turn on a switch and light comes forth, as long as all was well with civilization. There may be some badly cut firewood for a fireplace that gives little heat, maybe enough for an hour or two. There may be an extra pound of hamburger and salad mix or a loaf of bread, bottled water for a day or two, the proper wine for beef and fish, but that's all. Most people don't allow the thought that civilization sometimes is ephemeral and so don't plan for a time when the lights don't shine and the water doesn't flow.

My neighborhood, today so far away, is different, and not usually where people expected me to live. One former classmate, now going to law school, looked at the address in horror. "But there's no country club!" No, it's a working-class neighborhood, full of the middle class and older folks, the American flag on the polished stoop as a sign of more than one patriot, more than one veteran. Some of us could live in neighborhoods much fancier. We chose not to.

Our homes were small as were our needs. For some, these are homes for young people who were just starting out. For others, the homes were small, so we could have the freedom to travel, to prepare, to help others in need. There's grain stored in the basement or shop, and there's wood for a winter. There's dirt on our shoes and dirt on our machinery, signs of unflagging labor. We don't live so close that we are on top of another, but we know each other's names. Food travels up and down the street for the shut-ins, for the ill, and sometimes, to bring a smile to a friend.

Like anyone, in any neighborhood, we could experience jealousy and pride, but for the most part, it was the pride of freedom and liberty, and the jealousy of the freedoms that once existed, that we strive so hard to maintain. We laughed loudly, we cried silently, and our knees could be as scuffed from prayer as from when we performed a battlefield medic's surgery on a broken lawnmower as the decorative plastic goose in the neighbor's yard looked on with the expression that said, "You should have bought a John Deere."

Our possessions may be old, but they are well tended and work. What was broken was not replaced but was repaired, for we understand that quality is a function of dependability over time, not something simply pristine in its appearance. On many a night, the TV laid silent as we worked on into the late hours, prepping food, cleaning our tools, sometimes working with little more than strong black coffee and a will to endure.

Thoughts of my home fell behind me, as I continued my drive toward where I would lay my head tonight. Just a few more miles, heading out past the airport, and traffic was slowing. At an intersection with an island between lanes, there's a young man holding a sign that said "homeless, hungry, please help, god bless" none of the words capitalized. I notice $100+ tennis shoes, a newer high-end label coat, clean fingernails and a good haircut, the only mark of his "homelessness" being a couple of days' growth of beard.

A few blocks away there were numerous warehouse type businesses, for the shipping centers that are near the airport. There are many of them with "help wanted" signs posted by the roadways, hiring for the Christmas season and beyond at far more than minimum wage. When I lived here, I saw people leaving those places when the 3 o'clock shift got out, some on bicycles, even in the cold, some walking, toting a lunch pail, the nearest area of housing or bus stop a couple of miles away. Such are people who want to work and work hard, even if it meant a long trek in the dark in the cold air. I looked that kid with the sign right in the eye, kept the window rolled up, and started moving away.

On the opposite corner from the young man with the sign, competing with a bigger sign was a woman. Hers was a face void of expectations, sunken in, no meat on her bones, bad teeth and the pockmarks of a serious drug habit all over her face. She leaned against the stop sign; a rag doll held up simply by need and addiction. Her sign was just leaning against the pole, unreadable to me. She could have been twenty-three or sixty-three. If I gave her something, it would not buy food or care, only her next fix, which could kill her. I drove on, but this time, not easily and with a tear in my eye for a soul so ravaged.

I noticed a lot of new cars on the road. I looked down at the dashboard. My truck had 84,000 miles on it. Since my aunt left me the house and all I had to pay for was upkeep and taxes, I could afford to buy a new one. But I'm not going to; I'm learning to repair rather than replace things, to live on what I have, not what I want.

Before I left the city, I stopped at a big-box-mart type store to get some driveway salt, the local grocers having sold out with a forecast of a coming storm. I preferred to shop at the small locally owned stores, but I needed to get some before it got dark and the storm hit.

In line with my one item, I followed an older man, neatly dressed and groomed, buying just a few things, as he paid with some carefully folded dollar bills, slowly counted out. His shoulders were straight. He was a person who had probably never taken a handout but for the Social Security he paid into his whole life. He's not buying chips and soda and frozen meals. There's dried grain and beans and some apples, carrots and a couple of onions, powdered milk, no good coffee, just cheap tea and a small, inexpensive chuck roast, food he will likely stretch as long as is possible. His hands showed decades of hard work, his frame was thin, his stance was proud, even if all it could bear now was a hard and Spartan heritage.

This community, thank God, still has more people willing to work than people willing to take, and seeing him lifted my spirits after my walk through the store. He accidentally dropped some coins as he got something from his pocket. Then he leaned over and picked them up, taking his things as he slowly walked toward the parking lot. I caught up with him after paying for my purchase. "Sir, I think you dropped this too." He looked up at me and smiled but looked puzzled. I pressed several crisp and neatly folded twenties in his hand and rushed off with a "Merry Christmas" before he could stop me.

On my way home, even tired, and a bit cold, I knew I could enjoy the Christmas lights as I traveled through the suburbs on my way out of the city. I was sad to see that as I drove, I saw little of the true meaning of Christmas. There were few Nativity scenes, just Santa and elves, now that the nation had systematically tried to remove God from the tapestry of America, unobstructed by the persuasive power of His Word or His Church.

On Christmas as a child, I said a prayer of thanks to God, sang a song for baby Jesus, and attended both evening and morning services. Christmas morning, my brother and I enjoyed a few presents for which we felt both thankful and blessed. Now Christmas is all Santa and reindeer and "what will you give me" rather than stopping for a moment to thank the One that gave all. We built our country on that rock, that example of blood and strength and hope, the seeded capital of the all-enduring Spirit, and traded Him for fables to soothe the children into darkness.

I'm happy my small town still has a Nativity scene in the square and fellow officers that helped string up the lights. That was a scene one will never see on TV, on a reality show, on the news. It was simply a slice of a single day in small-town America as viewed from my eyes. This was America, not Europe, as much as some people want to make it like Europe. Here the land is vast and open, spurning confinement, unlike most of the small countries in Europe where you can't swing a cat without accidentally whacking a border guard. My grandparents on my mother's side immigrated here for a reason. Our ideas were revolutionary, our people strong, and opportunities existed if you worked very, very hard. You succeeded and failed by your personal initiative.

This land was my grandparents' America, and it is mine. It's people struggling, people hoping, people succeeding, people failing. People still dreaming of what it once was and what it still can be. Not just a Democracy, but an undefeated Democratic Republic, not undefeated because it was never challenged, but undefeated because it was bravely and firmly protected, shielded in its impeccable frailty.

We are more and more a nation divided of our view of what we expect of our country: entitlements and handouts from above and the freedom from want versus self-reliance, sacrifice, and the freedom to fail. Both sides of that particular coin may equally support and defend our country, but both differ greatly in what they expect back in return from its government. I know, looking at hands that are not uninitiated to either blood or courage, what I expect from my country. I don't expect the promise of success without effort. I expect my government to honor this country the same as those who protect her do. If those politicians need a reminder, it's called the Constitution.

As I drove, I saw signs that there are still many that believe as I do, in the qualities of hard work, responsibility, and helping neighbors who *will* help themselves. I am proud to be their neighbor. As I traveled through this city, into the small towns that circled it like stars, the signs of our economic overindulgence and the culture of entitlement are everywhere—in the small things that many would drive by without noticing, in others that most simply prefer to turn a blind eye to.

As I arrived in the driveway, I was grateful to live in this place that others would call "redneck," "backward," and "middle of nowhere," because there my values were respected.

Chapter 30

———✳———

*T*he smell of wood smoke was in the air this morning. Morning gave way to a thin cloud cover that draped over the landscape. They were so different than the clouds of summer, those enormous ones that race across the land, freer than those they cover, but without a home.

I liked having a home, even here beneath a burnished sky. From my upstairs office, I could see the street and the life upon it, in more than one direction. In the morning, the sun bursts forth in a seemingly swift show of light that stirs the shadows and the soul. In the evening, the copper light retires slowly, not diminished in size by the millions of years that it had born witness to the world, even as it seems to slow from the strain of all it has seen before vanishing for the night. Evelyn and I would sometimes just sit and watch it from the porch, a mug of tea in our hands, joined here in this place that is our safety.

From the end of the street comes a deep rumble, the whoosh of things being swept aside, a street sweeper making its way, releasing to the sky the smell of autumn's perfume, dirt, and smoke. I think back to the city, remembering more than the fun that I had, but remembering all of the areas, so poor in not just money but in hope. There in those neighborhoods I dared not travel, there were few leaves, gutters full of trash, which will not be swept away, as young men dispense out of blued barrels, their illusion of strength, there in a city where more than leaves will fall, as autumn turns into winter.

When I made the trip so many months ago to Chicago, during the Christmas season, I had time to have coffee with David. He was telling me he was now part of a Christian outreach group that provides prayer and support for young men and women incarcerated and in post-prison vocational education. I know it is good that he is part of that, bringing the love of Christ to hurting men and women, showing them who Jesus is and what He has done, but I worry about his safety as he travels.

I was glad he comes here to visit. Because I had little desire to return to the city to socialize, I'm happier to stay far away, away from the noise and the lights, here in a small town lined with ancient trees from which the leaves fall gently down. I love walking in the clean light, as neighbors rake yet another pile of leaves to burn, with a friendly wave, and a barking dog as I pass. I walk unchallenged and unfettered, breathing deep the sights and the smells of the day as I wait for the return of a young man who has become my best friend.

I decided to take Clyde out for one last walk before making my journal entry tonight. As I neared my home on the way back, I picked up a fistful of leaves with my free hand. I threw them in the air like a child at that moment, not merely a single soul that pales in the immensities beyond the created universe, but as my center, immortal even as my veins grow dark as the leaves do, there in those final years between birth and night.

Chapter 31

I don't have time for a journal entry, but it was a special weekend, and I need to write about it.

With help from my friend David, my uncle's Triumph is running. I should say, with my making sandwiches, while my friend David did most of the work. It was pouring down rain last weekend when he finished up, so I promised him a ride next time he came here to visit.

Fortunately, the vehicle was part of the trust that the house was in, so getting it registered in my name wasn't a huge hassle. We do have an attorney in town that pretty much specializes in everything. He at least keeps busy with that retired farmer that very loudly in the diner announces which kid he's leaving out of the will this week because of some perceived slight. I'm glad I went into law enforcement and not law; I would lose patience quickly with someone so unforgiving.

I'm not going to use the Triumph as my primary vehicle. I have seen too many accidents to want to be zipping around in a little red car the size of a skateboard all of the time, but in my uncle's memory, I will drive it enough to keep it running, my days of speeding to outrun my past long gone.

It was too nice of a day to not go for a drive out in the country. Unfortunately, I went a little farther than expected, and I found myself unsure as to where exactly I was. I could probably backtrack, but up ahead I saw a woman with a little roadside stand and a sign that said, "farm fresh eggs for sale."

As I approached her, enjoying a day out of uniform, just jeans and a warm sweater, she probably thought I looked twelve. She was an older woman who had seen some rough times, and there was sadness in her eyes that I once held in mine.

"Are you lost?" she asked.

Something about her, the sag of her shoulders, and the lost look in her eyes just spoke to me.

"Well I could use a hint on getting back to Brookdale, but I'm no longer lost. Can I tell you why?"

That was the first time I had ever witnessed for Jesus. I am not sure what I said, following the example for witnessing that Jesus gave as He talked to the women of Samaria. I shared my story, and I shared some scripture from a small Bible in my travel bag.

She explained she had lost her husband. Her kids didn't want to live out here near her, though they did invite her to join them in the big cities where they lived. She couldn't leave the house she'd shared with her husband for fifty years, even though she could barely tend to it all. I asked her if she had prayed about it.

"I think I forgot how."

With those words, we prayed together, and then I asked her to accept Christ in her life, here and now. With tears on her face, she did, the words of the Lord's Prayer coming back to her as I held her hands and she thanked Jesus for his forgiveness, asking Him to be her personal Savior.

I was rather nervous at that step, but until we ask the person to trust Christ as his or her Savior and Lord, our witness is not complete.

I left her a card from our church as well as my phone number and told her I'd be honored to give her a ride this Sunday if she would like to come to church with me.

But first, she had to draw this seasoned traveler a little map back to town.

Chapter 32

———————✳︎———————

J peeled wallpaper for most of the morning, sweat dripping down my forehead, landing on my tongue, tasting of the essence of me, salt and earth. I have to say I got a lot done, but it hurts to type this, oh Journal.

At first, the movements were enjoyable, the early evening light coming in not as dimness, but bright as silver, the remaining sunlight streaming through it, as if a sieve. For a while I enjoyed the repeated motions, as I scraped the paper from old walls, free of obligations but to this task, its unique sight and unique smell, reminiscent of old books in an ancient library. After about an hour, shaving the never quite vertical pieces of paper from walls that steadfastly hold on to it, as if it was all that was supporting its very structure, I was regretting not only my decision to tackle this job by myself but to own a home at all.

A glass of some cold water would be good, I thought. It would cool me off a bit while I take a rest. After that, it was time for another half hour of labor, followed by time for another break and some tea. At that point, it became not so much a task but a philosophical discourse with not just the house but me, seeing into the violated walls, not just a simple task of unpainted wood and sweat but the very existences of mortality and the doom of mere flesh.

When you wax philosophical while stripping wallpaper it's time just to stop for the night and have some chocolate especially after realizing that to finish you needed:

(a) a break,
(b) C4, or
(c) a professional.

I called it quits for the night and went and got a long shower. It was a wall in the living room; the paper removed to paint. I'd picked out a can at the local hardware store. It's a soothing color, like the vase that Evelyn gave me when I first moved in, a cool green resting place, that spot to where I always circle back, like a wheel, hubbed in that place that can't be placed on a map but steadfastly exists.

It's not as bad as the wallpaper at my neighbor Harry's house. In the kitchen is something that could only be described as "Olive Garden" on steroids, with flowering trellises, bright flowers, and grapes that looked as if they were bleeding O positive. And it covered the entire kitchen. In the bathroom and bedroom were also wallpaper cherubs that wound their way around the entire border of the master bed and bath. But when I heard Harry talk about his wife and how much she loved to decorate, I knew he found comfort in it, those pieces of her.

His house was near a big pond, with woods and corn fields behind him, but he was still close enough to town that he could walk to Main Street to eat at the diner if he wanted. I enjoy my evenings when I'm reading with him or playing board games with both him and Evelyn. For at least tonight, I'm going to stay home. I'm sore all over.

No one told me how hard wallpaper was to remove, though. I tried the usual methods, spray on "easy wallpaper remover" which was about as effective as Congress just before recess. I tried sheer force and heat. In sheer desperation, I resorted to muttering in my grandmother's native tongue (dear Lord, muttering in Swedish just *sounds* like you're swearing) but mostly it just took moisture and a tool sharper than muscle or wit. By the time I was halfway through the task, the wallpaper was Tokyo, and I was that giant lizard monster from the cheesy 50s movies.

Sometimes when we start something, we have no idea what it is going to entail. I'm not naturally "Miss Home Improvement," but it never stopped me. There is a photo of my dad and me that I still have. I'm probably four or five years old, in my little coveralls and painters cap "helping" my dad paint the house. I honestly had more paint on me than the house. He didn't criticize, though, letting me learn. During the last couple of years of his life, I did most of the basic house upkeep for him, since that day I came home and found Dad on a ladder, with the leaf blower, trying to blow leaves out of the gutters. I never expected to take the storage shed keys away from him before the car keys.

The serious stuff (plumbing/chimney) Dad paid for professionals to do, the little stuff I did for him there in his last year. There was a bar to grab onto in the shower if his blood pressure dropped. I installed new linoleum tiles in the kitchen, and those 1970s orange beaded "drapes" Grandma put up in the laundry room and one bath were replaced with some beautiful lace curtains found at a thrift store.

I also found homes for some of the clutter that made it difficult for him to navigate in the dark. I found a place for a few small but good chairs rarely used, as well as some tiny decorative tables. I understood navigating in the dark. One night when still in uniform, Clyde and I ran a cleaned pan that had held a meatloaf Evelyn made for me after a long day over to her house just as a severe storm hit. She insisted we stay the night rather than go home while lightning was flashing as the storm was forecasted to last a few hours. In the guest room was a man's suit rack—you know those waist-high contraptions that sit in a bedroom, holding your good clothes all neatly (as if you don't own a closet). Well, after bumping into that while trying to find the light switch, I thought we'd had a home invasion by a well-dressed dwarf, and almost put a round of .45 through it.

I found that I enjoyed the process of removing the wallpaper, even though it's back-breaking work. Perhaps I'm odd in this thought, but like some automobiles, I feel that an old house is a living thing, in how you care for it, react to it, trust it or hate it, simply accept it or love it. I occasionally come across one in late hours of the night that has burned to the ground with the force of fate's conflagration, and in my tired brain I wonder if it knew, like some centurion whose mind has gone — did you know what has happened to you, do you even know you have died?

The time and relationships with such things have served a purpose. I've done things I didn't think I was clever or strong enough to do. I learned some things one should *not* do. A bench vice works much better than your knees, and a Bush Hog can do many outdoor heavy tasks, perhaps not with the ease of explosives, but with better odds of my colleagues not showing up.

Now it's time for some pain reliever and sleep.

Chapter 33

————————※————————

*S*ometimes you think you can fly, only to be destined to drown.

And so we stay earthbound. We recall much of life as each year passes, candles on another cake, warm breath against the flames. What do you remember most, the best day of your life or your last regret?

The difference is profound.

I remember my dad, long after my mom and brother passed, and when their names were mentioned, he got this look of profound grief on his face, even as I've learned to get through the day as a stoic. He was a man who was not time's trinket and for him, my mom's death months before was like it was yesterday, even up until his own death reached out for him. He'd not have given up the experience of loving her, for any different outcome.

I remembered back more than two years ago when I came to this small town. I thought my heart was in pieces, not likely to heal. A fractured goodbye and the realization that the person I had cared for, who introduced me to his family, was not who I thought he was. I was left with just a rose, drying between two pages, the blood from an internal thorn tearing something loose inside, the print of nose against the glass of the school library where I leaned into it so the tears couldn't be seen. Afterward, I wondered if life was even worth living, there in that brief darkness before there was light.

I would not go down that path. That thought was only one moment of brief self-pity not intended to be action. I had a good cry and some chocolate and a glass of wine with my best gal friend followed by a full night's sleep. The next morning, we set out in her car, and as we drove around a haunted landscape, I realized that although I hurt, I *felt*, and that was a good thing.

Then, after another good night's sleep, I picked up the phone and called my best platonic guy friend from all of my teen years, one I used to spend hours on the phone with or online sharing geeky puns and jokes. Yes, David. I knew he would understand. "Daniel and I broke up," was all I said, and he listened, as he always did while I talked it out, and tried to put it behind me. In talking to him, I realized that as much as I hurt, it was more from the pain of abandonment. I wasn't in love with Daniel; he was just a handsome and witty constant in life. That helped me understand it better, but it didn't make the loss any less hurtful.

It wasn't the first time my heart had broken, and perhaps wouldn't be the last, but the feeling peeled something from me, like skin from an onion, leaving nerves exposed to a cold that bit with sharp teeth. It brought back a memory of that first loss of someone I loved and a memory of how I handled it. For that first time, when my heart broke, when I buried the first member of my family, I did what a lot of people do. I pushed everyone away, pushing my boundaries, driving too late and too fast, sober, but risking a traffic ticket or an accident. The speed was a distraction from the pain, the air parting like the Red Sea ahead of my vehicle, my only need to move on at maximum risk to my body and minimum risk to my soul.

I wanted nothing from the world but the ability to push through it without being touched. I talked little to people but much to the open road, whispering to it my regrets as I took a corner too fast, taking counsel with that great blue sky above.

You think that cheating death like that would make me feel alive, but for a time, it was a battle without passion, gray and colorless, with neither the urge to win nor the fear of losing, played out before an arena with no audience. I came within a few miles per hour of a final pronouncement more than once and found that I had nothing left to say.

The only sound was the sound of the wheels on the road, a sound that is like all other sounds of profound mystery, the lap of a wave upon a shore, the echo of taps, the whispers of a voice that spoke to you in dreams from an eternity away, heard but not comprehensible.

I lost out on a lot of life during that brief time.

I lost my compass, and somewhere in there, I wandered from the path of my faith in God.

When my boyfriend and I broke up, I was a bit older, and a little scar tissue and I weren't strangers. Losing your whole family within a few years of one another was worse than breaking up a budding relationship. I decided that I was going to open myself up to friends and get out and enjoy my life. I tossed out every silly little thing my ex-boyfriend Daniel had bought me and spent time with my friends, learning to laugh again, in fairly short order. On one of the rare days, that I let that last heartache get the better of me, one of those friends asked, "If you had to do it all again, knowing it would teach you how to feel again, would you?" I looked her and said, with no hesitation, "Yes."

After that phone call regarding the break-up I didn't meet up with David for a few months, but our talks continued with the usual chatter between people that share hobbies and books and a long history as friends. After I got settled in Aunt Ruby's home, we'd chat online, trying to see who could make up the worst pun, just having fun. Then one night he mentioned a date with a former classmate, one of the most beautiful girls on campus, and I felt something twist within my chest I hadn't felt before. I didn't say anything, not then, not on his next visit to see his cousin. I asked if he was bringing her and he just laughed and said, "That was just one date; her credit card, not Christ, is the center of her world." My mind shouted, "Yes! He's not seeing her anymore!"

The following summer, after many a visit to his Cousin Ezekiel's, he asked if I wanted to attend a state farm festival. He had enough points to get us two free motel rooms. Though they would be different hotels, due to the points he was using, they'd be close enough we could get a burger together afterward. I had known David since we were twelve, both of us choosing the same college and becoming fast friends there, and I knew I'd have a great time with him.

I touch the frame of the window next to the computer on which I now type; tracing it the way fingers trace a human backbone, there under the skin, in a silent perusal of that strength as I think back to that trip.

Clyde went to stay with Evelyn for the night; she had become the Mom I hadn't had in quite a while. The farm festival was so much fun, way more fun than some of the things we thought were cool to do in the city. We decided to get a quick burger once we got a chance to get cleaned up back at our respective hotels. He showed up at my door dressed in dress pants and a crisp shirt, and the burger joint I was expecting turned into an intimate, elegant bistro and a conversation about things much deeper than the night, things only hinted at, never spoken aloud.

Halfway through the meal, I thought, *Wow, this is a date.*

That was last summer, on a warm, clear day. That amazing man, my long-time friend, is now my husband of six months.

Because he asked.

How often do we stay silent, when we are searching, when we need help, when we are hurt? How often do we shut ourselves away when we want a cool touch upon the brow or a hand to help us up a steep slope? There is so much that can keep us from the truth of things, holding us in that toil of a heart's hesitation.

Sometimes it's pride; sometimes it's hurt. Sometimes it's history. Often it's the fear of being rejected. The safety stays on; the mouth remains closed, and while we think we are protecting ourselves, we're merely closing the door on life, one that can be as fixed as one of a prison. In doing so, sometimes we lose a friend, we lose an opportunity, or we lose on love — that improbable, inexplicable and sometimes bewildering thing that binds us together despite our blood, or through it.

One of the younger officers once lamented to me in a moment of vulnerability after a very late night on the job that his old high school crush was marrying someone else. I said, "Did you ever ask her out?" He said, "No. I knew she would say no; she was beautiful and popular, and I'm . . .," as he paused, accepting the words as he uttered them with an almost eager fatalism. That which makes something its truth also makes it its meaning. I should have offered comfort, but I remained silent, not knowing what to say.

So he and I just continued to work, in silence, our untrammeled feet taking us to a place rendered quiet not by solitude, but by a loss. We worked on, blind and deaf to any emotion but the gathering, and I realized I should have said something, with a smile, and a hug from a friend, not a colleague.

On a day when another birthday shortly loomed, I looked at what is around me, and how I almost lost it, lost me, simply by never taking the chance, listening to my doubts and not to my heart. For the past does have a way of coming back to us. You can fear it in silence, treating it as if you would have an unwanted dream, or you can learn from it, remembering it as a fine book, full of wonders and maybe random warfare, but as full of life as the landscape around you.

For what I've learned in my years on this planet, is the earth is simply a standing place, and how you look at what is around you is your loss or your gain.

The sky and water weld together without joint, the sun descending, touching the small pond down the street with a soundless hiss. Soon, the moon would spread over this place with the thick sheen of silver. I will catalog this day in memory with the living trees, the flowers planted by my aunt's hands, so still they appear to have been formed in stone, even to the smallest bud, the feather stroke of a tiny leaf.

I will soon be another year older, another day wiser. I could worry about it, or as I did on my last birthday, I could just smile as David put a single plumber's candle on my cake as he said, "There are more years than candles." With that we both laughed; a sound that could bend the trees and shake the fixed stars in the sky. I turned toward the door, where a blond young man stood with a smile, my dear friend Evelyn behind him with a wrapped package. With God, they are my strength and they are my family.

I wanted them both to be here to tell them our little family is expanding.

Chapter 34

———✳———

*D*ear Journal: life is getting busy, so you and I may have to have these little chats less and less. My husband is getting his business started up here in our home, which means a laptop in the kitchen until we can upgrade the electrical wiring in this old room upstairs. I'll have to make a few more entries before our baby is born.

As I watched my husband tonight, I thought about a man's shaving ritual. Men have shaved for centuries, even in the days of rampant beards, some men preferred to remain clean shaven. My brother had a small beard. With his red hair, build, and height he very much resembled a Viking, until cancer took 120 pounds off his frame, tempering his blade, honing his spirit, even as it strengthened his faith and trust in God.

This evening I happily watched my husband shave, as I gathered up some towels in the bathroom to be taken down to the laundry room. I remembered when my dad tried to grow a mustache once. It was in the mid-90s and was less than successful. Dad had fine, dark red hair that resulted in a mustache that came in thin and sparse. I remembered my mom looking at the outcome and trying her hardest not to giggle and failing to do so. Dad looked at her with a wry smile and shrugged and went back to the bathroom and shaved it off. Mom wasn't trying to belittle his efforts, her love fluttered over all of us like small wings, whisking away tears and brushing aside fears. She treated Dad the same way, but oh dear was that a sorry-looking mustache and even Dad realized it.

So from that day forward, each and every morning, my dad was in the bathroom shaving.

For most men, the morning shave is something they must do each and every day. It was done whether there was a houseful of kids bustling around or they were on their own.

Tonight, watching my husband shave brought back memories of my dad's ritual, which remained to the day he died. After he had a cup of coffee, he'd sit and read the Bible for a while and then the daily devotion from the little book our Lutheran church gave out. Then he'd shave. He never used an electric razor or any of the shave creams in a can. No, Dad always had a mug of fine soap, a high-quality brush, and a regular razor, with a straight razor when he wanted an extra close shave for a special occasion.

I remembered vividly back to some winter mornings, all of us dressing quickly, not so much that the house was cold, but hearts and blood and minds weren't quite awake yet, and the movement was with willful purpose until the chocolate milk or the caffeine kicked in. Dad would come through the kitchen from where he had his quiet time, giving my mom a kiss, the morning sun highlighting the freckles on her face, and then a kiss for each of us, still in our pajamas, our faces innocent of either guile or water.

While my brother and I tried to stay out of his way, he'd shave, the tiny half bath that was his bathroom, filling with steam. He was careful with the straight razor, pulling it over features as carefully as if they were oiled glass, rinsing the razor in hot water, as the dark stubble on his face brushed away like filings from a new gun barrel. I simply watched from the kitchen table, carefully and quietly. Dad was so intent on his task before he even drew down that sharpened blade in its first stroke, his attention was almost perceptible in the air, surrounding him as fragrance does, leaving a subtle impression of his intent long before the act was complete.

When he was done, he'd finish as he started, with a clean washcloth doused in extra hot water, laid on his face to steam it. Then he would finish with a splash of aftershave. There would be only a couple of bottles in the cabinet, his favorite being Old Spice.

I missed that smell, one that was both reassurance and comfort. I'm glad my husband has much the same ritual as Dad did, with the soap in a mug and a high-quality brush. He often shaved at night, after I've had my bubble bath, and as I curled up on the sofa with a small mug of chamomile tea, he would begin that ritual. He's shaved in dozens of hotels as he traveled for his IT business, the ritual much the same I imagined, yet there's something almost peaceful about the act performed in one's bathroom, in one's home, small rituals of sameness.

Many of us wander all over the world, the esteemed and the obscure, the bold and the invisible, earning beyond the oceans our riches, our scars, and our destiny. When we do go home, we are rendering an account; we are sweeping away those things we picked up that pull us down, as we surrounded ourselves with the familiar, with that which is cherished, that which is holy.

When he is done, he'll join me on the couch in his bathrobe, with a mug of tea of his own, the house quiet but for hundred-year-old sconces on the walls that lend the room an aura of timelessness and the cross that hung on the wall in my childhood home. We won't talk much but of family, of things in our home that need repair, or simply our day as we sit and stroke the flanks of an old black dog that lies beside us. Before we go to bed, we will pray, his hand in mine imparting love as well as strength as we bow our heads together. Such rituals are as fine as a blade, as comforting as stone. Shared, they are as bright and uplifting as the flash of sparks as dulled blade and stone meet.

Outside in the warm air, from a distance, there was a rumble. I remembered something about a severe storm warning this evening. I had better check the radar and see if we needed to get Clyde out to the yard before bedtime a little earlier than normal as that dog will not go out once there is the sound of thunder.

For now, I have just a few final thoughts to be captured here in words. So much has changed, this house having seen both the lives and the deaths of my family, walls still adorned with their photographs. So much gone, swirled down the drain with past and present tears. Still, I looked at the world as I did those long-ago mornings here as a child, carefully and quietly. And when my husband now stands behind me, after giving me a hug to let me know he's finished his tasks and wished for our evening-time talk and prayer, I breathed deep a familiar scent. It's Old Spice. On my husband it smells different than I remember on my dad; but it brings with it that same feeling as he gives me a kiss, tenderly on the top of my head as I type these words. In that moment of ritual, I'm at peace, safe, and loved, with a future that is too far away to fear.

In the distance, there is a flash of light against the sky as the wind begins to pick up.

Chapter 35

———————※———————

*I*t was the sound that woke Evelyn up.

It's one she knew that Rachel normally heard at the police station every morning at 11 A.M. unless there is severe weather forecast. It is a sound you don't want to hear any other time.

Especially at 3 o'clock in the morning.

At sixty-four years of age, she's lived through some tornados, though all of the large ones have gone north or south of town.

There is still a great danger if one touches down—even a small one can send a large tree into a home, down power lines, and damage homes. She has two things to do and do them quickly. The first is to get the key to her neighbor Harry's house, as she has one in case he's not well enough to let her in on her visits.

Then she grabs a blanket and a bag that contains a first aid kit, a flashlight, some protein bars and water. She's spent at least a few hours in the basement when the sirens went off in the past, and if she is trapped for any time if her house is hit, she will need some essentials. After getting Boo-Boo into the basement where she has a kennel she loves to sleep in that is under a cement-reinforced area Evelyn's husband put in as a makeshift storm shelter, she hurries out, making sure the dog is secure with food and water.

Lightning is still in the distance, so she knows she has a few minutes, but she doesn't think she has time to get Harry out of bed and over to her basement. They're going to have to hunker down in his. She prays Rachel and her husband heard the sirens as well as their other neighbor, Betty, the recently widowed woman a couple of doors down.

As she enters the house, she sees Harry asleep in his recliner, stretched out, and covered by a blanket. His evening's nursing aide likely left him there if he was soundly sleeping as he is often restless at night, and a sound night's sleep isn't always in his grasp.

She gently touches his shoulder, and as he opens his eyes, she says, "Harry, a tornado has been spotted nearby; we need to go to the basement." He looks at her and says, "I can't. I'm not strong enough for the stairs any longer."

Harry is twice the weight of Evelyn and a foot taller. There will be no carrying him.

Evelyn says, "OK, we're going to go to the master bathroom off your bedroom; that's in the center of the house."

Harry says, "Leave me, you go to the basement."

Evelyn says, "You are my friend and my brother in Christ, and I am *not* leaving you." Using his walker, they get moved to the bathroom. She helps him into the bathtub while she gets the cushions from his couch to place around him to offer some protection if a wall comes down, hoping that there's the strength of cement around his 1940s bathroom remodel, as was common at the time.

As she grabs more pillows, she sees the lights on from Rachel's basement. "Good," she thinks. "Those two kids are safely downstairs."

Outside, the darkness became even darker, if that were possible, a lowering of light that could almost be felt. It was if all the lights outside were on one switch and someone just turned them down. The wind was a steady push, rain hitting the ground outside like artillery fire.

She looks at Harry, and he's smiling. Evelyn asks, "How can you be smiling?" Harry responded, "I'd prayed I'd get to spend an evening's company with a beautiful woman; this just isn't how I planned it."

She knew he was just joking; he treated her as he would treat a daughter, and with great respect, but she appreciated him trying to take some of the fear from her.

The bedroom window outside rattled with the wind, almost shaking in its uneasiness. A faint burst of lightning had flashed into the bathroom before she closed the door, almost as if someone had shone a flashlight into a dark cistern, her gleaming eyes all it would see in return.

As the wind picked up to a howl, the little flip phone in her pocket rang.

"Evelyn, it's Rachel, we have the radar up and the news on with our little TV down here. There's a tornado headed right toward us, moving to the Northeast. It's not an F5, but it's big, and it's going to do some damage. Where are you?"

Evelyn said, "I couldn't get Harry to the basement, we're in the central bath, and I've got Harry in the tub covered with cushions."

Just then, there is a sound like she'd never heard before from behind the house, so much beyond the power of her reasoning that it was incomparable with any experience she'd had when storms rolled across the cornfields. The rain pours outside, in sheets, as a strip of gutter comes loose, beating itself against the side of the house as if the lone percussion to this night's music.

From outside there is a huge crash as she covers Harry's body with her own, her fears becoming one with prayer. "Dear Lord, we are old and have lived many good years. Watch over us, your children, or bring us home to your glory, but please keep the young people safe. We trust you in all things. Amen."

The air outside screams as if sucked through a tunnel when suddenly the lights went out leaving them with nothing but a roar of the wind that defies all hope.

Chapter 36

------------ ❋ ------------

*W*e don't have to speak for our intentions to be read. Speech seems like a simple thing, a coordination of muscle and bone, nerves and tongue, something within us, just as the ability to control and guide both weapon and machine lay slumbering within the wrists and hands. We can stay silent, but the words are still there.

Man experiences things of great magnitude and cannot speak of them at all. Artists or craftspersons create something that was part of them, honed into art or machine. On completion, they say no words, they call no one, and they simply put down their tool, their brush, and stare at their vision, incarnate.

Veterans come home from battle empty of all words, bound together by only that identical experience which they can never forget and dare not speak of, lest by speaking of darkness, they are wrapped in its chains. First responders and law-enforcement officers often relate as they too see so much death that never again, as long as they breathe, will they ever truly go to sleep alone.

Man experiences the mundane, the meaningless, tweeting and texting of it feverishly. It is as if, by doing so, inconsequential acts become more than the passing of time by the imminently bored. The words can uplift, but they can also sting like so many insects, their incessant noise, finally dimming to a hum.

We speak in different languages, and even when speaking the same language, we often don't communicate. Moreover, even when we do, we often don't truly mean what we say. Promises can be nothing more than words and oaths, empty air, especially when election times near, wherein contests of fierce and empty oratory are somehow, retroactively, supposed to make us believe, any more than they can make us forget.

We speak in the language of the past, chants unchanged in generations hanging in the air as God is placed into a golden cup, there underneath the eyes of angels. We speak in the language of silent prayer, calling upon God and our reserves, saying prayers without words, as we draw near our weapon as we enter what could be hell on earth.

Words can support, they can heal, with gentle utterance after a nightmare in the still of the night, the soothing voice that smooths the frayed edges of a day with nothing more than the touch of supple prose. Words can injure, cutting like a knife, discharging like a spark of electricity, those words, from someone we love, marking us always with their wounding.

Words, a movement of lips and tongue that can cause laughter or pain; that can divide or conquer. Even in a nation where English is the official language, in parts of our country, there are whole neighborhoods where you won't hear it spoken.

Sometimes one doesn't need to speak at all.

On any given day, tragedy and the earth collide, flood, tornado, the plunging of a mighty machine into a peaceful neighborhood. The details differ, but the response is always the same. When disaster strikes, the land itself turns mute and those who remain, stand simply as silent instruments unable to make a sound.

I didn't fully understand that until the tornado came through our town last night, leveling several homes a mile or so north, leaving others, like mine and most of my neighbors, miraculously standing. We were lucky, in that there were no deaths, the majority of the homes having basements and a good tornado warning system. As we came up from our basement, our house untouched but for a tree that took out the front porch, it was as if what I viewed was a completely different town.

Harry, my elderly friend from across the street, was on the sidewalk, Evelyn holding on to him, shaken but unhurt. Ezekiel and Miriam waved from down the block, his shop roof damaged but the structure intact. But just down from Harry's home, Betty, the widow that lives there stood in front of what remained of her house of sixty years. It was one set further back from the road than the others, the back portion of the house completely missing its roof and some walls, not even a photo of her failed dreams left where the wind rushed through those rooms. She cried silently, in the faded robe she fled in, as one of the neighbors came over and put her arms around her. Behind all of the homes across the street from us, there were so many trees downed, limbs flung through windows, shattering them as if they were thrown like a lance.

A young woman, her face growing older by the minute, stumbled from the walkout basement of the home that had sold when I moved in, a solitary figure, clutching only a stuffed animal, making a path toward what is known. Her brother, deployed in military service, was letting her live in his home to care for the place while she attended a community college in a town not too far from here. We beckoned her to come over to us, and though I am probably only ten years older than she, like Evelyn does with me, I hold her in a mother's protective embrace.

The older couple from the corner of the block lost a brand new outbuilding they had painstakingly constructed behind their house. They now could only look at the work of their sweat and tears strewn about for miles by the force of nature, the wind thick and warm, like blood spilled, pooling around what little remains. A lone tree stood among so many that were downed, torn out by the roots, its nervous branches bent down as if hoping not to be noticed.

173

The first responders arrived, standing for just a moment, still and mute, hands unmoving beneath the invisible stain of what was, always, needless blood. For just a moment they stopped, as if by whispered breath or the movement of disturbed air, what little remains, would crumble.

They gathered, moving in and around, the firefighters, emergency medical personnel, law-enforcement officers, wearing blue and black and yellow. Such garments, solemnly worn, exchanged for lives that used to be ordinary, worn as they shape something from chaos, coercing that terrible blood wind to give up a sound, the forlorn echo of someone who might have survived underneath the carnage. I waved at an officer I worked with, seeing the relief in his eyes that I was unhurt, feeling like I should be doing something more to help. I realized that I was still in shock as I held my neighbor to me to comfort as beneath my bathrobe my precious unborn child lay safe.

It's surprising how much noise there was in the silence, of hope, of grief, of disbelief. It was a sound which one could almost, but not quite, capture, receding like dwindling song until there were only the shadows and the quiet. And then a small voice, "Can anyone help me?" low and faint as the vespers of sleep. It came from a home that didn't have a walkout basement, and a tree had gone through the sunroom. I had been there, and that would have blocked the basement stairs. Hopefully, the person is fine and can get out once the tree was moved.

Survivors and saviors, moved without sound, sending a message as loudly to the heavens as if they were one voice. People were helped from the rubble, the injured accessed, the grief-stricken comforted as best as one could, if only by a touch that resonated straight to the heart, bypassing a brain that could not accept its fate. There were no teleprompters, there were no cue cards, and there were no words for boundless grief and regret. There was no language for this, no word, no sound; it's defiant and imminent life, holding on.

Chapter 37

It's hard to believe I've been in this house almost three years now, adding not just renovations, but a spouse, a life I always thought would be another's, not mine. As I make these notes in my journal, my husband is outside looking at a pile of stringers to rebuild the porch steps, as a man does when confronted by a creature that may sting or bite, and he cares for neither. He'll get it done, even if it takes a couple more weekends because we want it done right, not quickly, a concept foreign to many people.

The last couple of weeks have been busy, but as a community we have come together, getting the two homes that suffered the worst damage on our block repaired with community work parties, helping clean up the debris and the limbs that were down, planting new trees. We had a pancake breakfast over at the church to raise money for the widow that had the worst of the damage, and she is staying with Evelyn until the roof and walls are repaired and the wind and water damage clean-up is completed. I called the woman I had witnessed to, who now attends our church, after the tornado. She said it missed her place completely though she said the hens didn't lay eggs that next morning, as they were still stressed about being moved to a more secure coop.

There was a work party late last night at one of the badly damaged homes. We didn't hear much, but there was an assortment of trucks and tools and lights that twinkled from the tiny kitchen. I looked out as I was getting my house closed up for the night; I saw the black portrait of an evening smoker. He stood against the dreaming bloom of the moonlight beyond the back deck, while from the inside, the occasional sound of a child's laughter played on the night air liked the song of a randomly plucked string.

I watched the homeowner get ready to leave for the night, the house still too damaged to provide shelter. She sat in her car, not yet running, for the longest time, the backseat filled with some clothes, a few boxes, and her form unmoving and wooden, as if she had been loaded inanimate into the vehicle, where she waited for someone to transport everything somewhere warm and safe. She looked up only once, as if by looking she could volley her vision far and away, like the trajectory of a ball into a distance where her future was clear and known.

As I turned away from the window, I realized that we've gotten a lot done on the house this year, most of it improvements you won't notice. There was only one kitchen project that I had to hire someone to help with, but it was a steady bit of restoration, organization, and cleaning up.

Seeing the house unfold has been a pleasure, though I'm sure burglars will look through the front window, see all of the antiques, the sconces on the wall, no big flat-screen TV, and they'd probably walk away thinking a couple of elderly people live here. Though the kitchen cabinets were completely rebuilt, the walls re-plastered and painted, it still looks like a 40s kitchen. The only new decorative bits are my mom's Swedish horses and a jar of marbles I found in my brother's childhood bedroom, the ones we played with for years as children, crouched down like small gargoyles perched on the edge of the earth.

My brother and I were quietly and fiercely competitive, and a game of marbles, like any game, was approached like an act of war, though not as intensely, with the only fire being friendly. I can still recall his pale hands gently grasping the larger marble, poised for movement, while I watched like a hawk, to see if I could discern by draw of breath, by the pace of breath, by the dart of an eye, his intention. There were times he was so intent on the task; it seemed as if he ceased to breathe; only the sun is glinting on the marble in his hand, letting me know that time had not stopped.

The sun still glints on those marbles as you walk through the kitchen into the living room. As I look around, I note that the time could be the current year or it could be 1935. I like that sense of timelessness as I spend my work day dealing with the machining of lives and law. By the time I get home, I'm breathing slow and labored, like a man with a large weight on his chest. I walk into this house, make some tea, put on some music, and light a lamp, and the air goes out of my chest in a gentle whoosh. In that instant, I care nothing for politics, for work, or what is outside, only the slow dance of my evening with my husband and our four-legged rescued companion.

Still, at times like these, I missed my brother. He was family, and I loved him as deeply as he loved and defended me.

I remembered back to when my brother's home was readied for sale, and his things were organized after he died, as we sorted through those mementos we wished to keep and those things that could go to charity.

His home had no home computer and no TV. The furniture was old and much of it was hand restored. The house was in need of updating, but he preferred to do that himself, on his schedule, rather than pay someone with the fruits of his labor for tasks he could easily learn how to do himself. There, beneath a stopped clock, responsive now only to the last stroke of eternity, sat some tools for yet another project he'd never be able to wield them for to finish.

But despite the lack of modern conveniences, there was one large 80s tape player and a stereo, with both vinyl and tapes to go with it that he bought at a yard sale. In the last year of his life, he played music almost all day, everything from big band to 70s rock. All of those tapes were bundled up in the boxes and boxes to be sorted through after he was gone. Some of it made me cry, some of it made me smile, and the first thing I am going to ask him when I see him in Heaven is why he had a live flare gun on his nightstand.

That last night as we gathered up his things, I realized, that as different as we were in some ways, he being the fellow that always had a hundred friends, I being the one that only allowed a handful in close, we were very much alike, strong-willed and sometimes stubborn. I could almost smell the white smoke of the cigarettes he refused to quit smoking, even as cancer ate at him, watching it burning in the ashtray by his fingers, the smoke trailing out the window into the tattered, tumbling midnight.

My brother spent his brief adult years in service to his country, something he was very proud to do even as he sometimes disagreed with its leadership. He was quiet in his public opinions on such matters, but in private, with one another, he would discuss with a great passion those failures and omissions of those we as a country put in power, as well as our staunch support of those rights that would keep us from forced servitude. For he knew that with enough power, this carefully built world still contains within it the command to be seized, and we'd make sure we did all we could to lawfully keep that from happening.

His car bore an emblem of the US flag, and his shelf the Bible, and he refused to apologize for either. He had little interest in promotions to higher command, as he realized that although command was sometimes magic, it often contained an atmosphere of officialdom that seemed to staunch human endeavor and he was happier as a simple Machinist Mate, preferring his hands bloodied or dirtied to the false supremacy of paper and ink.

I'm glad I had those days and those memories; for my brother left an imprint of his life behind, one that's so similar to mine, that in the recognition of, I sometimes feel closer to him in death than our deep bond in life.

As the tools were put down as darkness was upon us this night, I looked up at the heavens. What captured my gaze were the unsteady stars, that if blown upon would tumble like large marbles in the sky and then brighten to small specks of light in a wet sheen, that I realized was the view through my tears.

With each small thing of his that are now part of my house, I realize that for all of us, midnight will come. However, I'm not going to let midnight be flung down upon me. I'm going to drag midnight along with me for the ride, as hammers are swung, and boards are bent, and God is our only salvation. In the end, it may not be done, but it will be started, and that, with the rest and the little death of sleep will be my escape and my reward. Then, when my body is finally free of sweat and the house is quiet, I'll sleep. It will be sleep without regret, in a slightly worse for wear home in which my God watches over me, and my defender lies quietly in the drawer, a round in the chamber.

Chapter 38

———————※———————

The morning was quiet; the phone silent; outside there was only the cool blessing of a Sunday afternoon.

Today was my mother's birthday, a day of quiet reflection and sorting through some old photographs that were put quickly into a box when she passed and never fully unpacked as the first time I did so I was so flooded with memory that I just lost it. Even with Mom gone, it was still a day I enjoyed as I looked through some of those pictures, while my husband was busy down the street helping with some of the continued clean-up efforts.

As I opened that box, I saw one photo of my brother and me. I am wearing a dress. I do *not* look happy. I have the same attitude about dresses to this day, though I will put one on for church as it pleases my husband. I'd rather be in jeans and a T-shirt.

Further down in the box, there was a photo of my parents. They looked to be in their thirties. They were in what looked like a saloon in cowboy gear, surrounded by others in cowboy gear while visiting friends in Montana. They looked like they were in their very own Roy Rogers movie and given the empties on the table; the cowboy gang had not just whiskey, but beer for their horses.

There were a few photos from my teen years, from the University. I looked at them in wonderment, not even being aware at the time, of my youth, or even of my face or form, it just being the vehicle to move me through my days. Did I note as I left my days of education behind that the passage had begun? Or did I simply float, detached from the earth, traveling solitary and swift through the skies, as if I were my own planet, the stars around me just distant distractions? We do that, when we're young, casting off that which seeks to hold us earthbound, moving onward in that circular solitude that is the egocentricity of youth. Once in a while, we meet others like ourselves, caught up in their destinies, appearing as nothing more than a speck on the horizon, then moving away. We have our futures, and they have theirs. We might join up in a brief flare of the sun that at the time seemed forever, but in looking back we saw it as brilliant and quick as a flash of a muzzle, as short as a fleeting dream.

I looked at other pictures; that first couple of years here in this small town, my life a landscape warmed by autumn's sun but not enough where it stirred either heat or movement, lazy, brandied days of rest and exploration wrapped in a mantle of warm clouds. My shoulders were hunched from a load of hope and regret, but the eyes, even as they had yet to show the tracings of laughter, were bright, looking upward, not looking back to the past, and seeing the future as an unlimited landscape, even one walked with a sidearm.

A photo fell to the floor of the little British car that I uncovered when I first cleared out the garage after my aunt's death. So many hours in that little convertible where I could find the true peace that is God, traveling down one of the country roads around here, my hair tossed about, words of praise on my lips. There would be days of the sublime sweetness that was the engine's song, as I murmured to it, coaxing it faster with words as delicate as a mother's touch.

I had learned to slow things down from my younger years, being called to crash scenes as an officer where the outcome of risk was too often young death. I wasn't the only officer with tears in his or her eyes at such events. I had learned that God sends the messengers of our fate to us, not in wrath against our presumptive push to heaven or the folly of our invention but to warn our ignorant hearts that we are sometimes just along for the ride. Now, when the speedometer gets to the speed limit in that little car, it goes no further,

I looked at a photo of my mother's form lying in her bed in her last days, having lived too long for the fire that was within her but not nearly long enough. In those last days, we did not talk of that coming death for it was already with us, interrupting us with its silence, taking up space between us as we attempted to draw close. Death would reveal the color and sound of its truth soon enough, even as we did our best to keep it from hogging the conversation.

On the dresser now—a small but heavy box within which is the weight of love. On top of it are three cartridges that one day rang out over a military cemetery when we laid my uncle in the ground. Each one was an embodiment of the truth that death has to have the last word. He died years before my aunt, yet the box was always free of dust, always tended, no matter how much time passed.

Where did the time go?

Today when the rain ceased, I went for a walk as Evelyn happily watched my son, James. We had asked her to do us the honor of being his grandmother as both my mother and my husband's mom were gone. She was with us at the hospital for his birth and would be a part of that baby's life and the life of any future children we were blessed with for as long as she lived. She cried tears of joy when we told her and said that on the day I moved in, she was sad for what she had lost, not knowing the riches the Lord had in store for her. I don't know if I will continue to work as a police officer once my family leave is over. Evelyn has offered to help out with him while I work, and my husband works from home, with minimal trips to the city to personally meet with clients. It would certainly give me a little time each day as he slept to write that book that Evelyn says is in me. That is something I'll let God present to me as His plan for us as we grow and pray together as a family.

I walk for a few minutes, looking slowly and carefully at others who were out enjoying the brief sun between storms. There were the young teens, wearing unsuitable clothing as some badge of honor, earbuds in, enclosed in a world that included only them. Not yet chastened by the sudden discovery of the insignificance of their youth, they flew above anything of weight, and I smiled, remembering too well those years, not wishing them back for any amount of gold.

There were the elderly, wisps of hair made silver by time's brushstroke, eyes crunched and crinkled with much laughter and tears as salty as the sea. They moved with some difficulty as if the earth grabbed onto their feet with each step; but they were moving, looking at something ahead that I could not see. I saw my friend Harry, out for a short walk with his nurse's aide, one of those neighbors that made me feel like part of a community again, and I waved.

There was a middle-aged couple out, both of them looking worried and stern, unhappy that their knees probably hurt, or that there's another door ding on the car, moving sad and still. Was it by choice, that some get this way as they approach their later years, seeing mortality up close, hearing the voices of the dead, wearied by their thoughts which used to fly with the rapidity and vividness of dreams?

There was another couple, even older, that I recognized from the house on the corner, but their age was invisible as they whizzed by me on their bicycles, laughing into the wind, daring time to catch up with them. They might have some sore muscles tonight but there might be whiskey and beer, shared without regrets.

Where did the time go?

We all might have years left, or we might have only days. I know how I want to live them.

My youth was behind me, and what was ahead was known only to God. I could go on through my day with awareness of that which can't be recaptured, or I could snatch with a hand of courage, a moment from the remorseless rush of time. I could hold in my hand the rescued fragments of life; holding so tight I could feel the prick of the sharpness drawing a drop of warm blood as I breathed deep this day. That would be my truth; that uncertain fate that binds us to one another, to the world.

Today is my time. I will look at the future and the end that waits for us all, not as a cry, but as a whisper from a great distance, heard not with fear but an encouragement to wrest everything of this day that I can.

Today, I will thank my Lord for these years on earth, trusting that my presence here will bring His message of love and forgiveness to my community, just as He loved and forgave me when I wandered from a righteous path.

Today, I will arrest within the space of a breath, that time.

For, here on these small town roads, Forgiveness and Faith are mine.